The Parish Register

George Crabbe

Contents

THE PARISH REGISTER

BY

George Crabbe

PART I.

Tum porro puer (ut saevis projectus ab undis,
Navita) nudus humi jacet infans indigus omni
Vitali auxilio, -
Vagituque locum lugubri complet, ut aequum est,
Cui tantum in vita restat transire malorum.
       LUCRETIUS, De Rerum Natura, lib.5

THE ARGUMENT.

The Village Register considered, as containing principally the
Annals of the Poor--State of the Peasantry as meliorated by
Frugality and Industry--The Cottage of an industrious Peasant; its
Ornaments--Prints and Books--The Garden; its Satisfactions--The
State of the Poor, when improvident and vicious--The Row or Street,
and its Inhabitants--The Dwellings of one of these--A Public House--
Garden and its Appendages--Gamesters; rustic Sharpers &c.--
Conclusion of the Introductory Part.

BAPTISMS.

The Child of the Miller's Daughter, and Relation of her Misfortune--
A frugal Couple; their Kind of Frugality--Plea of the Mother of a
natural Child; her Churching--Large Family of Gerard Ablett: his
apprehensions: Comparison between his state and that of the wealthy
Farmer his Master: his Consolation--An Old Man's Anxiety for an
Heir: the Jealousy of another on having many--Characters of the
Grocer Dawkins and his Friend; their different Kinds of
Disappointment--Three Infants named--An Orphan Girl and Village
School-mistress--Gardener's Child: Pedantry and Conceit of the
Father: his botanical Discourse: Method of fixing the Embryo-fruit
of Cucumbers--Absurd Effects of Rustic Vanity: observed in the
names of their Children--Relation of the Vestry Debate on a
Foundling: Sir Richard Monday--Children of various Inhabitants--The
poor Farmer--Children of a Profligate: his Character and Fate--
Conclusion.

The year revolves, and I again explore
The simple Annals of my Parish poor;
What Infant-members in my flock appear,
What Pairs I bless'd in the departed year;
And who, of Old or Young, or Nymphs or Swains,
Are lost to Life, its pleasures and its pains.
   No Muse I ask, before my view to bring
The humble actions of the swains I sing. -
How pass'd the youthful, how the old their days;
Who sank in sloth, and who aspired to praise;
Their tempers, manners, morals, customs, arts,
What parts they had, and how they 'mploy'd their parts;
By what elated, soothed, seduced, depress'd,
Full well I know-these Records give the rest.

Is there a place, save one the poet sees,
A land of love, of liberty, and ease;
Where labour wearies not, nor cares suppress
Th' eternal flow of rustic happiness;
Where no proud mansion frowns in awful state,
Or keeps the sunshine from the cottage-gate;
Where young and old, intent on pleasure, throng,
And half man's life is holiday and song?
Vain search for scenes like these! no view appears,
By sighs unruffled or unstain'd by tears;
Since vice the world subdued and waters drown'd,
Auburn and Eden can no more be found.

Hence good and evil mixed, but man has skill
And power to part them, when he feels the will!
Toil, care, and patience bless th' abstemious few,
Fear, shame, and want the thoughtless herd pursue.

Behold the Cot! where thrives th' industrious swain,
Source of his pride, his pleasure, and his gain;
Screen'd from the winter's wind, the sun's last ray
Smiles on the window and prolongs the day;
Projecting thatch the woodbine's branches stop,
And turn their blossoms to the casement's top:
All need requires is in that cot contain'd,
And much that taste untaught and unrestrain'd
Surveys delighted; there she loves to trace,
In one gay picture, all the royal race;
Around the walls are heroes, lovers, kings;
The print that shows them and the verse that sings.

Here the last Louis on his throne is seen,
And there he stands imprison'd, and his Queen;
To these the mother takes her child, and shows
What grateful duty to his God he owes;
Who gives to him a happy home, where he

Lives and enjoys his freedom with the free;
When kings and queens, dethroned, insulted, tried,
Are all these blessings of the poor denied.

    There is King Charles, and all his Golden Rules,
Who proved Misfortune's was the best of schools:
And there his Son, who, tried by years of pain,
Proved that misfortunes may be sent in vain.

    The Magic-mill that grinds the gran'nams young,
Close at the side of kind Godiva hung;
She, of her favourite place the pride and joy,
Of charms at once most lavish and most coy,
By wanton act the purest fame could raise,
And give the boldest deed the chastest praise.

    There stands the stoutest Ox in England fed;
There fights the boldest Jew, Whitechapel bred;
And here Saint Monday's worthy votaries live,
In all the joys that ale and skittles give.

    Now, lo! on Egypt's coast that hostile fleet,
By nations dreaded and by NELSON beat;
And here shall soon another triumph come,
A deed of glory in a deed of gloom;
Distressing glory! grievous boon of fate!
The proudest conquest at the dearest rate.

    On shelf of deal beside the cuckoo-clock,
Of cottage reading rests the chosen stock;
Learning we lack, not books, but have a kind
For all our wants, a meat for every mind.
The tale for wonder and the joke for whim,
The half-sung sermon and the half-groan'd hymn.
No need of classing; each within its place,
The feeling finger in the dark can trace;
"First from the corner, farthest from the wall,"
Such all the rules, and they suffice for all.

There pious works for Sunday's use are found;
Companions for that Bible newly bound;
That Bible, bought by sixpence weekly saved,
Has choicest prints by famous hands engraved;
Has choicest notes by many a famous head,
Such as to doubt have rustic readers led;
Have made them stop to reason WHY? and HOW?
And, where they once agreed, to cavil now.
Oh! rather give me commentators plain,
Who with no deep researches vex the brain;
Who from the dark and doubtful love to run,
And hold their glimmering tapers to the sun;
Who simple truth with nine-fold reasons back,
And guard the point no enemies attack.
    Bunyan's famed Pilgrim rests that shelf upon;
A genius rare but rude was honest John;
Not one who, early by the Muse beguiled,
Drank from her well the waters undefiled;
Not one who slowly gained the hill sublime,
Then often sipp'd and little at a time;
But one who dabbled in the sacred springs,
And drank them muddy, mix'd with baser things.
    Here to interpret dreams we read the rules,
Science our own! and never taught in schools;
In moles and specks we Fortune's gifts discern,
And Fate's fix'd will from Nature's wanderings learn.
    Of Hermit Quarll we read, in island rare,
Far from mankind and seeming far from care;
Safe from all want, and sound in every limb;
Yes! there was he, and there was care with him.
    Unbound and heap'd, these valued tomes beside,
Lay humbler works, the pedlar's pack supplied;
Yet these, long since, have all acquired a name:

The Wandering Jew has found his way to fame;
And fame, denied to many a labour'd song,
Crowns Thumb the Great, and Hickathrift the strong.
    There too is he, by wizard-power upheld,
Jack, by whose arm the giant-brood were quell'd:
His shoes of swiftness on his feet he placed;
His coat of darkness on his loins he braced;
His sword of sharpness in his hand he took,
And off the heads of doughty giants stroke:
Their glaring eyes beheld no mortal near;
No sound of feet alarm'd the drowsy ear;
No English blood their Pagan sense could smell,
But heads dropt headlong, wondering why they fell.
    These are the Peasant's joy, when, placed at ease,
Half his delighted offspring mount his knees.
    To every cot the lord's indulgent mind
Has a small space for garden-ground assign'd;
Here--till return of morn dismiss'd the farm -
The careful peasant plies the sinewy arm,
Warm'd as he works, and casts his look around
On every foot of that improving ground :
It is his own he sees; his master's eye
Peers not about, some secret fault to spy;
Nor voice severe is there, nor censure known; -
Hope, profit, pleasure,--they are all his own.
Here grow the humble cives, and, hard by them,
The leek with crown globose and reedy stem;
High climb his pulse in many an even row,
Deep strike the ponderous roots in soil below;
And herbs of potent smell and pungent taste,
Give a warm relish to the night's repast.
    Apples and cherries grafted by his hand,
And cluster'd nuts for neighbouring market stand.

Nor thus concludes his labour; near the cot,
The reed-fence rises round some fav'rite spot;
Where rich carnations, pinks with purple eyes,
Proud hyacinths, the least some florist's prize,
Tulips tall-stemm'd and pounced auriculas rise.
  Here on a Sunday-eve, when service ends,
Meet and rejoice a family of friends;
All speak aloud, are happy and are free,
And glad they seem, and gaily they agree.
What, though fastidious ears may shun the speech,
Where all are talkers, and where none can teach;
Where still the welcome and the words are old,
And the same stories are for ever told;
Yet theirs is joy that, bursting from the heart,
Prompts the glad tongue these nothings to impart;
That forms these tones of gladness we despise,
That lifts their steps, that sparkles in their eyes;
That talks or laughs or runs or shouts or plays,
And speaks in all their looks and all their ways.
  Fair scenes of peace! ye might detain us long,
But vice and misery now demand the song;
And turn our view from dwellings simply neat,
To this infected Row, we term our Street.
  Here, in cabal, a disputatious crew
Each evening meet; the sot, the cheat, the shrew;
Riots are nightly heard: --the curse, the cries
Of beaten wife, perverse in her replies;
While shrieking children hold each threat'ning hand,
And sometimes life, and sometimes food demand:
Boys, in their first-stol'n rags, to swear begin,
And girls, who heed not dress, are skill'd in gin:
Snarers and smugglers here their gains divide;
Ensnaring females here their victims hide;

And here is one, the Sibyl of the Row,
Who knows all secrets, or affects to know.
Seeking their fate, to her the simple run,
To her the guilty, theirs awhile to shun;
Mistress of worthless arts, depraved in will,
Her care unblest and unrepaid her skill,
Slave to the tribe, to whose command she stoops,
And poorer than the poorest maid she dupes.
　Between the road-way and the walls, offence
Invades all eyes and strikes on every sense;
There lie, obscene, at every open door,
Heaps from the hearth, and sweepings from the floor,
And day by day the mingled masses grow,
As sinks are disembogued and kennels flow.
　There hungry dogs from hungry children steal;
There pigs and chickens quarrel for a meal;
Their dropsied infants wail without redress,
And all is want and woe and wretchedness;
Yet should these boys, with bodies bronzed and bare,
High-swoln and hard, outlive that lack of care -
Forced on some farm, the unexerted strength,
Though loth to action, is compell'd at length,
When warm'd by health, as serpents in the spring,
Aside their slough of indolence they fling.
　Yet, ere they go, a greater evil comes -
See! crowded beds in those contiguous rooms;
Beds but ill parted, by a paltry screen
Of paper'd lath, or curtain dropt between;
Daughters and sons to yon compartments creep,
And parents here beside their children sleep:
Ye who have power, these thoughtless people part,
Nor let the ear be first to taint the heart.
　Come! search within, nor sight nor smell regard;

The true physician walks the foulest ward.
See on the floor, where frousy patches rest!
What nauseous fragments on yon fractured chest!
What downy dust beneath yon window-seat!
And round these posts that serve this bed for feet;
This bed where all those tatter'd garments lie,
Worn by each sex, and now perforce thrown by!
  See! as we gaze, an infant lifts its head,
Left by neglect and burrow'd in that bed;
The Mother-gossip has the love suppress'd
An infant's cry once waken'd in her breast;
And daily prattles, as her round she takes
(With strong resentment), of the want she makes.
  Whence all these woes?--From want of virtuous will,
Of honest shame, of time-improving skill;
From want of care t'employ the vacant hour,
And want of every kind but want of power.
  Here are no wheels for either wool or flax,
But packs of cards--made up of sundry packs;
Here is no clock, nor will they turn the glass,
And see how swift th' important moments pass;
Here are no books, but ballads on the wall,
Are some abusive, and indecent all;
Pistols are here, unpair'd; with nets and hooks,
Of every kind, for rivers, ponds, and brooks;
An ample flask, that nightly rovers fill
With recent poison from the Dutchman's still;
A box of tools, with wires of various size,
Frocks, wigs, and hats, for night or day disguise,
And bludgeons stout to gain or guard a prize.
  To every house belongs a space of ground,
Of equal size, once fenced with paling round;
That paling now by slothful waste destroyed,

Dead gorse and stumps of elder fill the void;
Save in the centre-spot, whose walls of clay
Hide sots and striplings at their drink or play:
Within, a board, beneath a tiled retreat,
Allures the bubble and maintains the cheat;
Where heavy ale in spots like varnish shows,
Where chalky tallies yet remain in rows;
Black pipes and broken jugs the seats defile,
The walls and windows, rhymes and reck'nings vile;
Prints of the meanest kind disgrace the door,
And cards, in curses torn, lie fragments on the floor.

  Here his poor bird th' inhuman Cocker brings,
Arms his hard heel and clips his golden wings;
With spicy food th' impatient spirit feeds,
And shouts and curses as the battle bleeds.
Struck through the brain, deprived of both his eyes,
The vanquished bird must combat till he dies;
Must faintly peck at his victorious foe,
And reel and stagger at each feeble blow:
When fallen, the savage grasps his dabbled plumes,
His blood-stain'd arms, for other deaths assumes;
And damns the craven-fowl, that lost his stake,
And only bled and perished for his sake.

  Such are our Peasants, those to whom we yield
Praise with relief, the fathers of the field;
And these who take from our reluctant hands
What Burn advises or the Bench commands.

  Our Farmers round, well pleased with constant gain,
Like other farmers, flourish and complain. -
These are our groups; our Portraits next appear,
And close our Exhibition for the year.

WITH evil omen we that year begin:
A Child of Shame,--stern Justice adds, of Sin,
Is first recorded;--I would hide the deed,
But vain the wish; I sigh, and I proceed:
And could I well th'instructive truth convey,
'Twould warn the giddy and awake the gay.

Of all the nymphs who gave our village grace,
The Miller's daughter had the fairest face:
Proud was the Miller; money was his pride;
He rode to market, as our farmers ride,
And 'twas his boast, inspired by spirits, there,
His favourite Lucy should be rich as fair;
But she must meek and still obedient prove,
And not presume, without his leave, to love.

A youthful Sailor heard him;--"Ha!" quoth he,
"This Miller's maiden is a prize for me;
Her charms I love, his riches I desire,
And all his threats but fan the kindling fire;
My ebbing purse no more the foe shall fill,
But Love's kind act and Lucy at the mill."

Thus thought the youth, and soon the chase began,
Stretch'd all his sail, nor thought of pause or plan:
His trusty staff in his bold hand he took,
Like him and like his frigate, heart of oak;
Fresh were his features, his attire was new;
Clean was his linen, and his jacket blue:
Of finest jean his trousers, tight and trim,
Brush'd the large buckle at the silver rim.

He soon arrived, he traced the village-green,
There saw the maid, and was with pleasure seen;
Then talk'd of love, till Lucy's yielding heart
Confess'd 'twas painful, though 'twas right to part.

"For ah! my father has a haughty soul;
Whom best he loves, he loves but to control;
Me to some churl in bargain he'll consign,
And make some tyrant of the parish mine:
Cold is his heart, and he with looks severe
Has often forced but never shed the tear;
Save, when my mother died, some drops expressed
A kind of sorrow for a wife at rest: -
To me a master's stern regard is shown,
I'm like his steed, prized highly as his own;
Stroked but corrected, threatened when supplied,
His slave and boast, his victim and his pride."

"Cheer up, my lass! I'll to thy father go,
The Miller cannot be the Sailor's foe;
Both live by Heaven's free gale, that plays aloud
In the stretch'd canvass and the piping shroud;
The rush of winds, the flapping sails above,
And rattling planks within, are sounds we love;
Calms are our dread; when tempests plough the deep,
We take a reef, and to the rocking sleep."

"Ha!" quoth the Miller, moved at speech so rash,
"Art thou like me? then where thy notes and cash?
Away to Wapping, and a wife command,
With all thy wealth, a guinea in thine hand;
There with thy messmates quaff the muddy cheer,
And leave my Lucy for thy betters here."

"Revenge! revenge!" the angry lover cried,
Then sought the nymph, and "Be thou now my bride."
Bride had she been, but they no priest could move
To bind in law the couple bound by love.

What sought these lovers then by day by night?
But stolen moments of disturb'd delight;
Soft trembling tumults, terrors dearly prized,

Transports that pain'd, and joys that agonised;
Till the fond damsel, pleased with lad so trim,
Awed by her parent, and enticed by him,
Her lovely form from savage power to save,
Gave--not her hand--but ALL she could she gave.

   Then came the day of shame, the grievous night,
The varying look, the wandering appetite;
The joy assumed, while sorrow dimm'd the eyes,
The forced sad smiles that follow'd sudden sighs;
And every art, long used, but used in vain,
To hide thy progress, Nature, and thy pain.

   Too eager caution shows some danger's near,
The bully's bluster proves the coward's fear;
His sober step the drunkard vainly tries,
And nymphs expose the failings they disguise.

   First, whispering gossips were in parties seen,
Then louder Scandal walk'd the village--green;
Next babbling Folly told the growing ill,
And busy Malice dropp'd it at the mill.

   "Go! to thy curse and mine," the Father said,
"Strife and confusion stalk around thy bed;
Want and a wailing brat thy portion be,
Plague to thy fondness, as thy fault to me; -
Where skulks the villain?" -

                    "On the ocean wide
My William seeks a portion for his bride." -

   "Vain be his search; but, till the traitor come,
The higgler's cottage be thy future home;
There with his ancient shrew and care abide,
And hide thy head,--thy shame thou canst not hide."

   Day after day was pass'd in pains and grief;
Week follow'd week,--and still was no relief:
Her boy was born--no lads nor lasses came

To grace the rite or give the child a name;
Nor grave conceited nurse, of office proud,
Bore the young Christian roaring through the crowd:
In a small chamber was my office done,
Where blinks through paper'd panes the setting sun;
Where noisy sparrows, perch'd on penthouse near,
Chirp tuneless joy, and mock the frequent tear;
Bats on their webby wings in darkness move,
And feebly shriek their melancholy love.
  No Sailor came; the months in terror fled!
Then news arrived--He fought, and he was DEAD!
  At the lone cottage Lucy lives, and still
Walks for her weekly pittance to the mill;
A mean seraglio there her father keeps,
Whose mirth insults her, as she stands and weeps;
And sees the plenty, while compell'd to stay,
Her father's pride, become his harlot's prey.
  Throughout the lanes she glides, at evening's close,
And softly lulls her infant to repose;
Then sits and gazes, but with viewless look,
As gilds the moon the rippling of the brook;
And sings her vespers, but in voice so low,
She hears their murmurs as the waters flow:
And she too murmurs, and begins to find
The solemn wanderings of a wounded mind.
Visions of terror, views of woe succeed,
The mind's impatience, to the body's need;
By turns to that, by turns to this a prey,
She knows what reason yields, and dreads what madness may.
  Next, with their boy, a decent couple came,
And call'd him Robert, 'twas his father's name;
Three girls preceded, all by time endear'd,
And future births were neither hoped nor fear'd:

Blest in each other, but to no excess,
Health, quiet, comfort, form'd their happiness;
Love all made up of torture and delight,
Was but mere madness in this couple's sight:
Susan could think, though not without a sigh,
If she were gone, who should her place supply;
And Robert, half in earnest, half in jest,
Talk of her spouse when he should be at rest:
Yet strange would either think it to be told,
Their love was cooling or their hearts were cold.
Few were their acres,--but, with these content,
They were, each pay-day, ready with their rent:
And few their wishes--what their farm denied,
The neighbouring town, at trifling cost, supplied.
If at the draper's window Susan cast
A longing look, as with her goods she pass'd,
And, with the produce of the wheel and churn,
Bought her a Sunday--robe on her return;
True to her maxim, she would take no rest,
Till care repaid that portion to the chest:
Or if, when loitering at the Whitsun-fair,
Her Robert spent some idle shillings there;
Up at the barn, before the break of day,
He made his labour for th' indulgence pay:
Thus both--that waste itself might work in vain -
Wrought double tides, and all was well again.
   Yet, though so prudent, there were times of joy,
(The day they wed, the christening of the boy.)
When to the wealthier farmers there was shown
Welcome unfeign'd, and plenty like their own;
For Susan served the great, and had some pride
Among our topmost people to preside:
Yet in that plenty, in that welcome free,

There was the guiding nice frugality,
That, in the festal as the frugal day,
Has, in a different mode, a sovereign sway;
As tides the same attractive influence know,
In the least ebb and in their proudest flow;
The wise frugality, that does not give
A life to saving, but that saves to live;
Sparing, not pinching, mindful though not mean,
O'er all presiding, yet in nothing seen.

   Recorded next a babe of love I trace!
Of many loves, the mother's fresh disgrace. -

   "Again, thou harlot! could not all thy pain,
All my reproof, thy wanton thoughts restrain?"

   "Alas! your reverence, wanton thoughts, I grant,
Were once my motive, now the thoughts of want;
Women, like me, as ducks in a decoy,
Swim down a stream, and seem to swim in joy.
Your sex pursue us, and our own disdain;
Return is dreadful, and escape is vain.
Would men forsake us, and would women strive
To help the fall'n, their virtue might revive."

   For rite of churching soon she made her way,
In dread of scandal, should she miss the day: -
Two matrons came! with them she humbly knelt,
Their action copied and their comforts felt,
From that great pain and peril to be free,
Though still in peril of that pain to be;
Alas! what numbers, like this amorous dame,
Are quick to censure, but are dead to shame!

   Twin-infants then appear; a girl, a boy,
Th' overflowing cup of Gerard Ablett's joy:
One had I named in every year that passed
Since Gerard wed! and twins behold at last!

Well pleased, the bridegroom smiled to hear--"A vine
Fruitful and spreading round the walls be thine,
And branch-like be thine offspring!"--Gerard then
Look'd joyful love, and softly said "Amen."
Now of that vine he'd have no more increase,
Those playful branches now disturb his peace:
Them he beholds around his tables spread,
But finds, the more the branch, the less the bread;
And while they run his humble walls about,
They keep the sunshine of good humour out.

   Cease, man, to grieve! thy master's lot survey,
Whom wife and children, thou and thine obey;
A farmer proud, beyond a farmer's pride,
Of all around the envy or the guide;
Who trots to market on a steed so fine,
That when I meet him, I'm ashamed of mine;
Whose board is high upheaved with generous fare,
Which five stout sons and three tall daughters share.
Cease, man, to grieve, and listen to his care.

   A few years fled, and all thy boys shall be
Lords of a cot, and labourers like thee:
Thy girls unportion'd neighb'ring youths shall lead
Brides from my church, and thenceforth thou art freed:
But then thy master shall of cares complain,
Care after care, a long connected train;
His sons for farms shall ask a large supply,
For farmers' sons each gentle miss shall sigh;
Thy mistress, reasoning well of life's decay,
Shall ask a chaise, and hardly brook delay;
The smart young cornet, who with so much grace
Rode in the ranks and betted at the race,
While the vex'd parent rails at deed so rash,
Shall d**n his luck, and stretch his hand for cash.

Sad troubles, Gerard! now pertain to thee,
When thy rich master seems from trouble free;
But 'tis one fate at different times assign'd,
And thou shalt lose the cares that he must find.
    "Ah!" quoth our village Grocer, rich and old,
"Would I might one such cause for care behold!"
To whom his Friend, "Mine greater bliss would be,
Would Heav'n take those my spouse assigns to me."
    Aged were both, that Dawkins, Ditchem this,
Who much of marriage thought, and much amiss;
Both would delay, the one, till--riches gain'd,
The son he wish'd might be to honour train'd;
His Friend--lest fierce intruding heirs should come,
To waste his hoard and vex his quiet home.
    Dawkins, a dealer once, on burthen'd back
Bore his whole substance in a pedlar's pack;
To dames discreet, the duties yet unpaid,
His stores of lace and hyson he convey'd:
When thus enriched, he chose at home to stop,
And fleece his neighbours in a new-built shop;
Then woo'd a spinster blithe, and hoped, when wed,
For love's fair favours and a fruitful bed.
Not so his Friend;--on widow fair and staid
He fix'd his eye, but he was much afraid;
Yet woo'd; while she his hair of silver hue
Demurely noticed, and her eye withdrew:
Doubtful he paused--"Ah! were I sure," he cried,
No craving children would my gains divide;
Fair as she is, I would my widow take,
And live more largely for my partner's sake."
With such their views some thoughtful years they pass'd,
And hoping, dreading, they were bound at last.
And what their fate? Observe them as they go,

Comparing fear with fear and woe with woe.
"Humphrey!" said Dawkins, "envy in my breast
Sickens to see thee in thy children blest:
They are thy joys, while I go grieving home
To a sad spouse, and our eternal gloom:
We look despondency; no infant near,
To bless the eye or win the parent's ear;
Our sudden heats and quarrels to allay,
And soothe the petty sufferings of the day:
Alike our want, yet both the want reprove;
Where are, I cry, these pledges of our love?
When she, like Jacob's wife, makes fierce reply,
Yet fond--Oh! give me children, or I die:
And I return--still childless doom'd to live,
Like the vex'd patriarch--Are they mine to give?
Ah! much I envy thee thy boys, who ride
On poplar branch, and canter at thy side;
And girls, whose cheeks thy chin's fierce fondness know,
And with fresh beauty at the contact glow."
   "Oh! simple friend," said Ditchem, "wouldst thou gain
A father's pleasure by a husband's pain?
Alas! what pleasure--when some vig'rous boy
Should swell thy pride, some rosy girl thy joy;
Is it to doubt who grafted this sweet flower,
Or whence arose that spirit and that power?
   "Four years I've wed; not one has passed in vain;
Behold the fifth! behold a babe again!
My wife's gay friends th' unwelcome imp admire,
And fill the room with gratulation dire:
While I in silence sate, revolving all
That influence ancient men, or that befall;
A gay pert guest--Heav'n knows his business--came;
A glorious boy! he cried, and what the name?

Angry I growl'd,--My spirit cease to tease,
Name it yourselves,--Cain, Judas, if you please;
His father's give him,--should you that explore,
The devil's or yours: --I said, and sought the door.
My tender partner not a word or sigh
Gives to my wrath, nor to my speech reply;
But takes her comforts, triumphs in my pain,
And looks undaunted for a birth again."

Heirs thus denied afflict the pining heart,
And thus afforded, jealous pangs impart;
Let, therefore, none avoid, and none demand
These arrows number'd for the giant's hand.

Then with their infants three, the parents came,
And each assign'd--'twas all they had--a name;
Names of no mark or price; of them not one
Shall court our view on the sepulchral stone,
Or stop the clerk, th' engraven scrolls to spell,
Or keep the sexton from the sermon bell.

An orphan-girl succeeds: ere she was born
Her father died, her mother on that morn:
The pious mistress of the school sustains
Her parents' part, nor their affection feigns,
But pitying feels: with due respect and joy,
I trace the matron at her loved employ;
What time the striplings, wearied e'en with play,
Part at the closing of the summer's day,
And each by different path returns the well-known way
Then I behold her at her cottage-door,
Frugal of light;--her Bible laid before,
When on her double duty she proceeds,
Of time as frugal--knitting as she reads:
Her idle neighbours, who approach to tell
Some trifling tale, her serious looks compel

To hear reluctant,--while the lads who pass,
In pure respect, walk silent on the grass:
Then sinks the day, but not to rest she goes,
Till solemn prayers the daily duties close.
But I digress, and lo! an infant train
Appear, and call me to my task again.
  "Why Lonicera wilt thou name thy child?"
I ask the Gardener's wife, in accents mild:
"We have a right," replied the sturdy dame; -
And Lonicera was the infant's name.
If next a son shall yield our Gardener joy,
Then Hyacinthus shall be that fair boy;
And if a girl, they will at length agree
That Belladonna that fair maid shall be.
  High-sounding words our worthy Gardener gets,
And at his club to wondering swains repeats;
He then of Rhus and Rhododendron speaks,
And Allium calls his onions and his leeks;
Nor weeds are now, for whence arose the weed,
Scarce plants, fair herbs, and curious flowers proceed,
Where Cuckoo-pints and Dandelions sprung
(Gross names had they our plainer sires among),
There Arums, there Leontodons we view,
And Artemisia grows where wormwood grew.
  But though no weed exists his garden round,
From Rumex strong our Gardener frees his ground,
Takes soft Senecio from the yielding land,
And grasps the arm'd Urtica in his hand.
  Not Darwin's self had more delight to sing
Of floral courtship, in th' awaken'd Spring,
Than Peter Pratt, who simpering loves to tell
How rise the Stamens, as the Pistils swell;
How bend and curl the moist-top to the spouse,

And give and take the vegetable vows;
How those esteem'd of old but tips and chives,
Are tender husbands and obedient wives;
Who live and love within the sacred bower, -
That bridal bed, the vulgar term a flower.

   Hear Peter proudly, to some humble friend,
A wondrous secret, in his science, lend: -
"Would you advance the nuptial hour and bring
The fruit of Autumn with the flowers of Spring;
View that light frame where Cucumis lies spread,
And trace the husbands in their golden bed,
Three powder'd Anthers;--then no more delay,
But to the stigma's tip their dust convey;
Then by thyself, from prying glance secure,
Twirl the full tip and make your purpose sure;
A long-abiding race the deed shall pay,
Nor one unblest abortion pine away."

   T'admire their Mend's discourse our swains agree,
And call it science and philosophy.

   "'Tis good, 'tis pleasant, through th' advancing year,
To see unnumbered growing forms appear;
What leafy-life from Earth's broad bosom rise!
What insect myriads seek the summer skies!
What scaly tribes in every streamlet move;
What plumy people sing in every grove!
All with the year awaked to life, delight, and love.
Then names are good; for how, without their aid,
Is knowledge, gain'd by man, to man convey'd?
But from that source shall all our pleasures flow?
Shall all our knowledge be those names to know?
Then he, with memory blest, shall bear away
The palm from Grew, and Middleton, and Ray:
No! let us rather seek, in grove and field,

What food for wonder, what for use they yield;
Some just remark from Nature's people bring,
And some new source of homage for her King.
   Pride lives with all; strange names our rustics give
To helpless infants, that their own may live;
Pleased to be known, they'll some attention claim,
And find some by-way to the house of fame.
   The straightest furrow lifts the ploughman's art,
The hat he gained has warmth for head and heart;
The bowl that beats the greater number down
Of tottering nine-pins, gives to fame the clown;
Or, foil'd in these, he opes his ample jaws,
And lets a frog leap down, to gain applause;
Or grins for hours, or tipples for a week,
Or challenges a well-pinch'd pig to squeak:
Some idle deed, some child's preposterous name,
Shall make him known, and give his folly fame.
   To name an infant meet our village sires,
Assembled all as such event requires;
Frequent and full, the rural sages sate,
And speakers many urged the long debate, -
Some harden'd knaves, who roved the country round,
Had left a babe within the parish bound. -
First, of the fact they question'd--"Was it true?"
The child was brought--"What then remained to do?"
"Was't dead or living?" This was fairly proved, -
'Twas pinched, it roar'd, and every doubt removed.
Then by what name th' unwelcome guest to call
Was long a question, and it posed them all;
For he who lent it to a babe unknown,
Censorious men might take it for his own:
They look'd about, they gravely spoke to all,
And not one Richard answer'd to the call.

Next they inquired the day, when, passing by,
Th' unlucky peasant heard the stranger's cry:
This known,--how food and raiment they might give
Was next debated--for the rogue would live;
At last, with all their words and work content,
Back to their homes the prudent vestry went,
And Richard Monday to the workhouse sent.
   There was he pinched and pitied, thump'd and fed,
And duly took his beatings and his bread;
Patient in all control, in all abuse,
He found contempt and kicking have their use:
Sad, silent, supple; bending to the blow,
A slave of slaves, the lowest of the low;
His pliant soul gave way to all things base,
He knew no shame, he dreaded no disgrace.
It seem'd, so well his passions he suppress'd,
No feeling stirr'd his ever-torpid breast;
Him might the meanest pauper bruise and cheat,
He was a footstool for the beggar's feet;
His were the legs that ran at all commands;
They used on all occasions Richard's hands:
His very soul was not his own; he stole
As others order'd, and without a dole;
In all disputes, on either part he lied,
And freely pledged his oath on either side;
In all rebellions Richard joined the rest,
In all detections Richard first confess'd;
Yet, though disgraced, he watched his time so well,
He rose in favour when in fame he fell;
Base was his usage, vile his whole employ,
And all despised and fed the pliant boy.
At length "'Tis time he should abroad be sent,"
Was whispered near him,--and abroad he went;

One morn they call'd him, Richard answer'd not;
They deem'd him hanging, and in time forgot, -
Yet miss'd him long, as each throughout the clan
Found he "had better spared a better man."
   Now Richard's talents for the world were fit,
He'd no small cunning, and had some small wit;
Had that calm look which seem'd to all assent,
And that complacent speech which nothing meant:
He'd but one care, and that he strove to hide -
How best for Richard Monday to provide.
Steel, through opposing plates, the magnet draws,
And steely atoms culls from dust and straws;
And thus our hero, to his interest true,
Gold through all bars and from each trifle drew;
But still more surely round the world to go,
This fortune's child had neither friend nor foe.
   Long lost to us, at last our man we trace, -
"Sir Richard Monday died at Monday Place:"
His lady's worth, his daughter's, we peruse,
And find his grandsons all as rich as Jews:
He gave reforming charities a sum,
And bought the blessings of the blind and dumb;
Bequeathed to missions money from the stocks,
And Bibles issued from his private box;
But to his native place severely just,
He left a pittance bound in rigid trust; -
Two paltry pounds, on every quarter's-day,
(At church produced) for forty loaves should pay;
A stinted gift that to the parish shows
He kept in mind their bounty and their blows!
   To farmers three, the year has given a son,
Finch on the Moor, and French, and Middleton.
Twice in this year a female Giles I see,

A Spalding once, and once a Barnaby: -
A humble man is HE, and when they meet,
Our farmers find him on a distant seat;
There for their wit he serves a constant theme, -
"They praise his dairy, they extol his team,
They ask the price of each unrivall'd steed,
And whence his sheep, that admirable breed.
His thriving arts they beg he would explain,
And where he puts the money he must gain.
They have their daughters, but they fear their friend
Would think his sons too much would condescend: -
They have their sons who would their fortunes try,
But fear his daughters will their suit deny."
So runs the joke, while James, with sigh profound,
And face of care, looks moveless on the ground;
His cares, his sighs, provoke the insult more,
And point the jest--for Barnaby is poor.
   Last in my list, five untaught lads appear;
Their father dead, compassion sent them here, -
For still that rustic infidel denied
To have their names with solemn rite applied:
His, a lone house, by Deadman's Dyke-way stood;
And his a nightly haunt, in Lonely-wood:
Each village inn has heard the ruffian boast,
That he believed "in neither God nor ghost;
That when the sod upon the sinner press'd,
He, like the saint, had everlasting rest;
That never priest believed his doctrines true,
But would, for profit, own himself a Jew,
Or worship wood and stone, as honest heathen do;
That fools alone on future worlds rely,
And all who die for faith deserve to die."
   These maxims,--part th' Attorney's Clerk profess'd,

His own transcendent genius found the rest.
Our pious matrons heard, and, much amazed,
Gazed on the man, and trembled as they gazed;
And now his face explored, and now his feet,
Man's dreaded foe in this bad man to meet:
But him our drunkards as their champion raised,
Their bishop call'd, and as their hero praised:
Though most, when sober, and the rest, when sick,
Had little question whence his bishopric.

But he, triumphant spirit! all things dared;
He poach'd the wood, and on the warren snared;
'Twas his, at cards, each novice to trepan,
And call the want of rogues "the rights of man;"
Wild as the winds he let his offspring rove,
And deem'd the marriage-bond the bane of love.

What age and sickness, for a man so bold,
Had done, we know not;--none beheld him old;
By night, as business urged, he sought the wood; -
The ditch was deep,--the rain had caused a flood, -
The foot-bridge fail'd,--he plunged beneath the deep,
And slept, if truth were his, th'eternal sleep.

These have we named; on life's rough sea they sail,
With many a prosperous, many an adverse gale!
Where passion soon, like powerful winds, will rage,
And prudence, wearied, with their strength engage:
Then each, in aid, shall some companion ask,
For help or comfort in the tedious task;
And what that help--what joys from union flow,
What good or ill, we next prepare to show;
And row, meantime, our weary bark to shore,
As Spenser his--but not with Spenser's oar.[1]

---

1 Allusions of this kind are to be found in the Fairy Queen. See the end of the First Book, and other places.

PART II.

Nubere si qua voles, quamvis properabitis ambo,
Differ; habent parvae commoda magna morae.
OVID, Fasti, lib.iii.

MARRIAGES.

Previous Consideration necessary: yet not too long Delay--Imprudent
Marriage of old Kirk and his Servant--Comparison between an ancient
and youthful Partner to a young Man--Prudence of Donald the
Gardener--Parish Wedding: the compelled Bridegroom: Day of
Marriage, how spent--Relation of the Accomplishments of Phoebe
Dawson, a rustic Beauty: her Lover: his Courtship: their
Marriage--Misery of Precipitation--The wealthy Couple: Reluctance
in the Husband; why?--Unusually fair Signatures in the Register:
the common Kind--Seduction of Lucy Collins by Footman Daniel: her
rustic Lover: her Return to him--An ancient Couple: Comparisons on
the Occasion--More pleasant View of Village Matrimony: Farmers
celebrating the Day of Marriage: their Wives--Reuben and Rachael, a
happy Pair: an example of prudent Delay--Reflections on their State
who were not so prudent, and its Improvement towards the Termination
of Life: an old Man so circumstanced--Attempt to seduce a Village

Beauty: Persuasion and Reply: the Event.
DISPOSED to wed, e'en while you hasten, stay;
There's great advantage in a small delay:
Thus Ovid sang, and much the wise approve
This prudent maxim of the priest of Love;
If poor, delay for future want prepares,
And eases humble life of half its cares;
If rich, delay shall brace the thoughtful mind,
T'endure the ills that e'en the happiest find:
Delay shall knowledge yield on either part,
And show the value of the vanquish'd heart;
The humours, passions, merits, failings prove,
And gently raise the veil that's worn by Love;
Love, that impatient guide!--too proud to think
Of vulgar wants, of clothing, meat, and drink,
Urges our amorous swains their joys to seize,
And then, at rags and hunger frighten'd, flees:
Yet not too long in cold debate remain;
Till age refrain not--but if old, refrain.
  By no such rule would Gaffer Kirk be tried;
First in the year he led a blooming bride,
And stood a wither'd elder at her side.
Oh! Nathan! Nathan! at thy years trepann'd,
To take a wanton harlot by the hand!
Thou, who wert used so tartly to express
Thy sense of matrimonial happiness,
Till every youth, whose banns at church were read,
Strove not to meet, or meeting, hung his head;
And every lass forebore at thee to look,
A sly old fish, too cunning for the hook;
And now at sixty, that pert dame to see,
Of all thy savings mistress, and of thee;
Now will the lads, rememb'ring insults past,

Cry, "What, the wise one in the trap at last!"
  Fie! Nathan! fie! to let an artful jade
The close recesses of thine heart invade;
What grievous pangs! what suffering she'll impart!
And fill with anguish that rebellious heart;
For thou wilt strive incessantly, in vain,
By threatening speech thy freedom to regain:
But she for conquest married, nor will prove
A dupe to thee, thine anger or thy love;
Clamorous her tongue will be: --of either sex,
She'll gather friends around thee and perplex
Thy doubtful soul;--thy money she will waste
In the vain ramblings of a vulgar taste;
And will be happy to exert her power,
In every eye, in thine, at every hour.
  Then wilt thou bluster--"No! I will not rest,
And see consumed each shilling of my chest:"
Thou wilt be valiant--"When thy cousins call,
I will abuse and shut my door on all:"
Thou wilt be cruel!--"What the law allows,
That be thy portion, my ungrateful spouse!
Nor other shillings shalt thou then receive;
And when I die--What! may I this believe?
Are these true tender tears? and does my Kitty grieve?
Ah! crafty vixen, thine old man has fears;
But weep no more! I'm melted by thy tears;
Spare but my money; thou shalt rule ME still,
And see thy cousins: --there! I burn the will."
  Thus, with example sad, our year began,
A wanton vixen and a weary man;
But had this tale in other guise been told,
Young let the lover be, the lady old,
And that disparity of years shall prove

No bane of peace, although some bar to love:
'Tis not the worst, our nuptial ties among,
That joins the ancient bride and bridegroom young; -
Young wives, like changing winds, their power display
By shifting points and varying day by day;
Now zephyrs mild, now whirlwinds in their force,
They sometimes speed, but often thwart our course;
And much experienced should that pilot be,
Who sails with them on life's tempestuous sea.
But like a trade-wind is the ancient dame,
Mild to your wish and every day the same;
Steady as time, no sudden squalls you fear,
But set full sail and with assurance steer;
Till every danger in your way be past,
And then she gently, mildly breathes her last;
Rich you arrive, in port awhile remain,
And for a second venture sail again.
  For this, blithe Donald southward made his way,
And left the lasses on the banks of Tay;
Him to a neighbouring garden fortune sent,
Whom we beheld, aspiringly content:
Patient and mild he sought the dame to please,
Who ruled the kitchen and who bore the keys.
Fair Lucy first, the laundry's grace and pride,
With smiles and gracious looks, her fortune tried;
But all in vain she praised his "pawky eyne,"
Where never fondness was for Lucy seen:
Him the mild Susan, boast of dairies, loved,
And found him civil, cautious, and unmoved:
From many a fragrant simple, Catherine's skill
Drew oil and essence from the boiling still;
But not her warmth, nor all her winning ways,
From his cool phlegm could Donald's spirit raise:

Of beauty heedless, with the merry mute,
To Mistress Dobson he preferr'd his suit;
There proved his service, there address'd his vows,
And saw her mistress,--friend,--protectress,--spouse;
A butler now, he thanks his powerful bride,
And, like her keys, keeps constant at her side.
　Next at our altar stood a luckless pair,
Brought by strong passions and a warrant there;
By long rent cloak, hung loosely, strove the bride,
From every eye, what all perceived, to hide,
While the boy-bridegroom, shuffling in his pace,
Now hid awhile and then exposed his face;
As shame alternately with anger strove,
The brain confused with muddy ale, to move
In haste and stammering he perform'd his part,
And look'd the rage that rankled in his heart;
(So will each lover inly curse his fate,
Too soon made happy and made wise too late:)
I saw his features take a savage gloom,
And deeply threaten for the days to come.
Low spake the lass, and lisp'd and minced the while,
Look'd on the lad, and faintly tried to smile;
With soften'd speech and humbled tone she strove
To stir the embers of departed love:
While he, a tyrant, frowning walk'd before,
Felt the poor purse, and sought the public door,
She sadly following, in submission went,
And saw the final shilling foully spent;
Then to her father's hut the pair withdrew,
And bade to love and comfort long adieu!
　Ah! fly temptation, youth, refrain! refrain!
I preach for ever; but I preach in vain!
　Two summers since, I saw at Lammas Fair

The sweetest flower that ever blossom'd there,
When Phoebe Dawson gaily cross'd the Green,
In haste to see, and happy to be seen:
Her air, her manners, all who saw admired;
Courteous though coy, and gentle though retired;
The joy of youth and health her eyes display'd,
And ease of heart her every look convey'd;
A native skill her simple robes express'd,
As with untutor'd elegance she dress'd;
The lads around admired so fair a sight,
And Phoebe felt, and felt she gave, delight.
Admirers soon of every age she gain'd,
Her beauty won them and her worth retain'd;
Envy itself could no contempt display,
They wish'd her well, whom yet they wish'd away.
Correct in thought, she judged a servant's place
Preserved a rustic beauty from disgrace;
But yet on Sunday-eve, in freedom's hour,
With secret joy she felt that beauty's power,
When some proud bliss upon the heart would steal,
That, poor or rich, a beauty still must feel.
  At length the youth ordain'd to move her breast,
Before the swains with bolder spirit press'd;
With looks less timid made his passion known,
And pleased by manners most unlike her own;
Loud though in love, and confident though young;
Fierce in his air, and voluble of tongue;
By trade a tailor, though, in scorn of trade,
He served the 'Squire, and brush'd the coat he made.
Yet now, would Phoebe her consent afford,
Her slave alone, again he'd mount the board;
With her should years of growing love be spent,
And growing wealth;--she sigh'd and look'd consent.

Now, through the lane, up hill, and 'cross the green:
(Seen by but few, and blushing to be seen -
Dejected, thoughtful, anxious, and afraid,)
Led by the lover, walk'd the silent maid;
Slow through the meadows roved they, many a mile,
Toy'd by each bank, and trifled at each stile;
Where, as he painted every blissful view,
And highly colour'd what he strongly drew,
The pensive damsel, prone to tender fears,
Dimm'd the false prospect with prophetic tears.-
Thus pass'd th' allotted hours, till lingering late,
The lover loiter'd at the master's gate;
There he pronounced adieu! and yet would stay,
Till chidden--soothed--entreated--forced away;
He would of coldness, though indulged, complain,
And oft retire, and oft return again;
When, if his teasing vex'd her gentle mind,
The grief assumed compell'd her to be kind!
For he would proof of plighted kindness crave,
That she resented first, and then forgave;
And to his grief and penance yielded more
Than his presumption had required before.
  Ah! fly temptation, youth; refrain! refrain!
Each yielding maid and each presuming swain!
  Lo! now with red rent cloak and bonnet black,
And torn green gown loose hanging at her back,
One who an infant in her arms sustains,
And seems in patience striving with her pains;
Pinch'd are her looks, as one who pines for bread,
Whose cares are growing--and whose hopes are fled;
Pale her parch'd lips, her heavy eyes sunk low,
And tears unnoticed from their channels flow;
Serene her manner, till some sudden pain

Frets the meek soul, and then she's calm again; -
Her broken pitcher to the pool she takes,
And every step with cautious terror makes;
For not alone that infant in her arms,
But nearer cause, her anxious soul alarms.
With water burthen'd, then she picks her way,
Slowly and cautious, in the clinging clay;
Till, in mid-green, she trusts a place unsound,
And deeply plunges in th' adhesive ground;
Thence, but with pain, her slender foot she takes,
While hope the mind as strength the frame forsakes;
For when so full the cup of sorrow grows,
Add but a drop, it instantly o'erflows.
And now her path, but not her peace, she gains,
Safe from her task, but shivering with her pains;
Her home she reaches, open leaves the door,
And placing first her infant on the floor,
She bares her bosom to the wind, and sits,
And sobbing struggles with the rising fits:
In vain they come, she feels the inflating grief,
That shuts the swelling bosom from relief;
That speaks in feeble cries a soul distress'd,
Or the sad laugh that cannot be repress'd.
The neighbour-matron leaves her wheel and flies
With all the aid her poverty supplies;
Unfee'd, the calls of Nature she obeys,
Not led by profit, not allur'd by praise,
And waiting long, till these contentions cease,
She speaks of comfort, and departs in peace.

   Friend of distress! the mourner feels thy aid;
She cannot pay thee, but thou wilt be paid.
But who this child of weakness, want, and care?
'Tis Phoebe Dawson, pride of Lammas Fair;

Who took her lover for his sparkling eyes,
Expressions warm, and love-inspiring lies:
Compassion first assail'd her gentle heart,
For all his suffering, all his bosom's smart:
"And then his prayers! they would a savage move,
And win the coldest of the sex to love:" -
But ah! too soon his looks success declared,
Too late her loss the marriage-rite repair'd;
The faithless flatterer then his vows forgot,
A captious tyrant or a noisy sot:
If present, railing, till he saw her pain'd;
If absent, spending what their labours gain'd;
Till that fair form in want and sickness pined,
And hope and comfort fled that gentle mind.
    Then fly temptation, youth; resist, refrain!
Nor let me preach for ever and in vain!
    Next came a well-dress'd pair, who left their coach,
And made, in long procession, slow approach;
For this gay bride had many a female friend,
And youths were there, this favour'd youth t'attend:
Silent, nor wanting due respect, the crowd
Stood humbly round, and gratulation bow'd;
But not that silent crowd, in wonder fix'd,
Not numerous friends, who praise and envy mix'd,
Nor nymphs attending near to swell the pride
Of one more fair, the ever-smiling bride;
Nor that gay bride, adorn'd with every grace,
Nor love nor joy triumphant in her face,
Could from the youth's sad signs of sorrow chase:
Why didst thou grieve? wealth, pleasure, freedom thine;
Vex'd it thy soul, that freedom to resign?
Spake Scandal truth? "Thou didst not then intend
So soon to bring thy wooing to an end?"

Or, was it, as our prating rustics say,
To end as soon, but in a different way?
'Tis told thy Phillis is a skilful dame,
Who play'd uninjured with the dangerous flame;
That, while, like Lovelace, thou thy coat display'd,
And hid the snare for her affection laid,
Thee, with her net, she found the means to catch,
And at the amorous see-saw won the match:
Yet others tell, the Captain fix'd thy doubt;
He'd call thee brother, or he'd call thee out: -
But rest the motive--all retreat too late,
Joy like thy bride's should on thy brow have sate;
The deed had then appear'd thine own intent,
A glorious day, by gracious fortune sent,
In each revolving year to be in triumph spent.
Then in few weeks that cloudy brow had been
Without a wonder or a whisper seen;
And none had been so weak as to inquire,
"Why pouts my Lady?" or "Why frowns the Squire?"
  How fair these names, how much unlike they look
To all the blurr'd subscriptions in my book:
The bridegroom's letters stand in row above,
Tapering yet stout, like pine-trees in his grove;
While free and fine the bride's appear below,
As light and slender as her jasmines grow.
Mark now in what confusion stoop or stand
The crooked scrawls of many a clownish hand;
Now out, now in, they droop, they fall, they rise,
Like raw recruits drawn forth for exercise;
Ere yet reform'd and modelled by the drill,
The free-born legs stand striding as they will.
  Much have I tried to guide the fist along,
But still the blunderers placed their blottings wrong:

Behold these marks uncouth! how strange that men
Who guide the plough should fail to guide the pen:
For half a mile the furrows even lie;
For half an inch the letters stand awry; -
Our peasants, strong and sturdy in the field,
Cannot these arms of idle students wield:
Like them, in feudal days, their valiant lords
Resign'd the pen and grasp'd their conqu'ring swords;
They to robed clerks and poor dependent men
Left the light duties of the peaceful pen;
Nor to their ladies wrote, but sought to prove,
By deeds of death, their hearts were fill'd with love.

   But yet, small arts have charms for female eyes;
Our rustic nymphs the beau and scholar prize;
Unletter'd swains and ploughmen coarse they slight,
For those who dress, and amorous scrolls indite.

   For Lucy Collins happier days had been,
Had Footman Daniel scorn'd his native green,
Or when he came an idle coxcomb down,
Had he his love reserved for lass in town;
To Stephen Hill she then had pledged her truth, -
A sturdy, sober, kind, unpolish'd youth:
But from the day, that fatal day she spied
The pride of Daniel, Daniel was her pride.
In all concerns was Stephen just and true;
But coarse his doublet was and patch'd in view,
And felt his stockings were, and blacker than his shoe;
While Daniel's linen all was fine and fair, -
His master wore it, and he deign'd to wear:
(To wear his livery, some respect might prove;
To wear his linen, must be sign of love:)
Blue was his coat, unsoil'd by spot or stain;
His hose were silk, his shoes of Spanish grain;

A silver knot his breadth of shoulder bore;
A diamond buckle blazed his breast before -
Diamond he swore it was! and show'd it as he swore;
Rings on his fingers shone; his milk-white hand
Could pick-tooth case and box for snuff command:
And thus, with clouded cane, a fop complete,
He stalk'd, the jest and glory of the street,
Join'd with these powers, he could so sweetly sing,
Talk with such toss, and saunter with such swing;
Laugh with such glee, and trifle with such art,
That Lucy's promise fail'd to shield her heart.

   Stephen, meantime, to ease his amorous cares,
Fix'd his full mind upon his farm's affairs;
Two pigs, a cow, and wethers half a score,
Increased his stock, and still he look'd for more.
He, for his acres few, so duly paid,
That yet more acres to his lot were laid:
Till our chaste nymphs no longer felt disdain,
And prudent matrons praised the frugal swain;
Who thriving well, through many a fruitful year,
Now clothed himself anew, and acted overseer.

   Just then poor Lucy, from her friend in town
Fled in pure fear, and came a beggar down;
Trembling, at Stephen's door she knocked for bread, -
Was chidden first, next pitied, and then fed;
Then sat at Stephen's board, then shared in Stephen's bed:
All hope of marriage lost in her disgrace,
He mourns a flame revived, and she a love of lace.

   Now to be wed a well-match'd couple came;
Twice had old Lodge been tied, and twice the dame;
Tottering they came and toying, (odious scene!)
And fond and simple, as they'd always been.
Children from wedlock we by laws restrain;

Why not prevent them when they're such again?
Why not forbid the doting souls to prove
Th' indecent fondling of preposterous love?
In spite of prudence, uncontroll'd by shame,
The amorous senior woos the toothless dame,
Relating idly, at the closing eve,
The youthful follies he disdains to leave;
Till youthful follies wake a transient fire,
When arm in arm they totter and retire.
  So a fond pair of solemn birds, all day
Blink in their seat and doze the hours away;
Then by the moon awaken'd, forth they move,
And fright the songsters with their cheerless love;
So two sear trees, dry, stunted, and unsound,
Each other catch, when dropping to the ground:
Entwine their withered arms 'gainst wind and weather,
And shake their leafless heads and drop together:
So two cold limbs, touch'd by Galvani's wire,
Move with new life, and feel awaken'd fire;
Quivering awhile, their flaccid forms remain,
Then turn to cold torpidity again.
  "But ever frowns your Hymen? man and maid,
Are all repenting, suffering, or betray'd?"
Forbid it, Love! we have our couples here
Who hail the day in each revolving year:
These are with us, as in the world around;
They are not frequent, but they may be found.
  Our farmers too, what though they fail to prove,
In Hymen's bonds, the tenderest slaves of love,
(Nor, like those pairs whom sentiment unites,
Feel they the fervour of the mind's delights;)
Yet coarsely kind and comfortably gay,
They heap the board and hail the happy day:

And though the bride, now freed from school, admits,
Of pride implanted there, some transient fits;
Yet soon she casts her girlish flights aside,
And in substantial blessings rest her pride.
No more she moves in measured steps; no more
Runs, with bewilder'd ear, her music o'er;
No more recites her French the hinds among,
But chides her maidens in her mother-tongue;
Her tambour-frame she leaves and diet spare,
Plain work and plenty with her house to share;
Till, all her varnish lost in few short years,
In all her worth the farmer's wife appears.
  Yet not the ancient kind; nor she who gave
Her soul to gain--a mistress and a slave:
Who, not to sleep allow'd the needful time;
To whom repose was loss, and sport a crime;
Who, in her meanest room (and all were mean),
A noisy drudge, from morn till night was seen; -
But she, the daughter, boasts a decent room,
Adorned with carpet, formed in Wilton's loom;
Fair prints along the paper'd wall are spread;
There, Werter sees the sportive children fed,
And Charlotte, here, bewails her lover dead.
  'Tis here, assembled, while in space apart
Their husbands, drinking, warm the opening heart,
Our neighbouring dames, on festal days, unite,
With tongues more fluent and with hearts as light;
Theirs is that art, which English wives alone
Profess--a boast and privilege their own;
An art it is where each at once attends
To all, and claims attention from her friends,
When they engage the tongue, the eye, the ear,
Reply when listening, and when speaking hear:

The ready converse knows no dull delays,
"But double are the pains, and double be the praise."
  Yet not to those alone who bear command
Heaven gives a heart to hail the marriage band;
Among their servants, we the pairs can show,
Who much to love and more to prudence owe:
Reuben and Rachel, though as fond as doves,
Were yet discreet and cautious in their loves;
Nor would attend to Cupid's wild commands,
Till cool reflection bade them join their hands:
When both were poor, they thought it argued ill
Of hasty love to make them poorer still;
Year after year, with savings long laid by,
They bought the future dwelling's full supply;
Her frugal fancy cull'd the smaller ware,
The weightier purchase ask'd her Reuben's care;
Together then their last year's gain they threw,
And lo! an auction'd bed, with curtains neat and new.
  Thus both, as prudence counsell'd, wisely stay'd,
And cheerful then the calls of Love obeyed:
What if, when Rachel gave her hand, 'twas one
Embrown'd by Winter's ice and Summer's sun ?
What if, in Reuben's hair the female eye
Usurping grey among the black could spy?
What if, in both, life's bloomy flush was lost,
And their full autumn felt the mellowing frost?
Yet time, who blow'd the rose of youth away,
Had left the vigorous stem without decay;
Like those tall elms in Farmer Frankford's ground,
They'll grow no more,--but all their growth is sound;
By time confirm'd and rooted in the land,
The storms they've stood, still promise they shall stand.
  These are the happier pairs, their life has rest,

Their hopes are strong, their humble portion blest.
While those more rash to hasty marriage led,
Lament th' impatience which now stints their bread:
When such their union, years their cares increase,
Their love grows colder, and their pleasures cease;
In health just fed, in sickness just relieved;
By hardships harass'd and by children grieved;
In petty quarrels and in peevish strife
The once fond couple waste the spring of life;
But when to age mature those children grown,
Find hopes and homes and hardships of their own,
The harass'd couple feel their lingering woes
Receding slowly till they find repose.
Complaints and murmurs then are laid aside,
(By reason these subdued, and those by pride;)
And, taught by care, the patient man and wife
Agree to share the bitter-sweet of life;
(Life that has sorrow much and sorrow's cure,
Where they who most enjoy shall much endure:)
Their rest, their labours, duties, sufferings, prayers,
Compose the soul, and fit it for its cares;
Their graves before them and their griefs behind,
Have each a med'cine for the rustic mind;
Nor has he care to whom his wealth shall go,
Or who shall labour with his spade and hoe;
But as he lends the strength that yet remains,
And some dead neighbour on his bier sustains,
(One with whom oft he whirl'd the bounding flail,
Toss'd the broad coit, or took the inspiring ale,)
"For me," (he meditates,) "shall soon be done
This friendly duty, when my race be run;
'Twas first in trouble as in error pass'd,
Dark clouds and stormy cares whole years o'ercast,

But calm my setting day, and sunshine smiles at last:
My vices punish'd and my follies spent,
Not loth to die, but yet to-live content,
I rest:"--then casting on the grave his eye,
His friend compels a tear, and his own griefs a sigh.
   Last on my list appears a match of love,
And one of virtue;--happy may it prove! -
Sir Edward Archer is an amorous knight,
And maidens chaste and lovely shun his sight;
His bailiff's daughter suited much his taste,
For Fanny Price was lovely and was chaste;
To her the Knight with gentle looks drew near,
And timid voice assumed to banish fear: -
"Hope of my life, dear sovereign of my breast,
Which, since I knew thee, knows not joy nor rest;
Know, thou art all that my delighted eyes,
My fondest thoughts, my proudest wishes prize;
And is that bosom--(what on earth so fair!)
To cradle some coarse peasant's sprawling heir,
To be that pillow which some surly swain
May treat with scorn and agonise with pain?
Art thou, sweet maid, a ploughman's wants to share,
To dread his insult, to support his care;
To hear his follies, his contempt to prove,
And (oh! the torment!) to endure his love;
Till want and deep regret those charms destroy,
That time would spare, if time were pass'd in joy?
With him, in varied pains, from morn till night,
Your hours shall pass; yourself a ruffian's right;
Your softest bed shall be the knotted wool;
Your purest drink the waters of the pool;
Your sweetest food will but your life sustain,
And your best pleasure be a rest from pain;

While, through each year, as health and strength abate,
You'll weep your woes and wonder at your fate;
And cry, 'Behold,' as life's last cares come on,
'My burthens growing when my strength is gone.'
  "Now turn with me, and all the young desire,
That taste can form, that fancy can require;
All that excites enjoyment, or procures
Wealth, health, respect, delight, and love, are yours:
Sparkling, in cups of gold, your wines shall flow,
Grace that fair hand, in that dear bosom glow;
Fruits of each clime, and flowers, through all the year
Shall on your walls and in your walks appear:
Where all beholding, shall your praise repeat,
No fruit so tempting and no flower so sweet:
The softest carpets in your rooms shall lie,
Pictures of happiest love shall meet your eye,
And tallest mirrors, reaching to the floor,
Shall show you all the object I adore;
Who, by the hands of wealth and fashion dress'd,
By slaves attended and by friends caress'd,
Shall move, a wonder, through the public ways,
And hear the whispers of adoring praise.
Your female friends, though gayest of the gay,
Shall see you happy, and shall, sighing, say,
While smother'd envy rises in the breast, -
'Oh! that we lived so beauteous and so blest!'
  "Come, then, my mistress, and my wife; for she
Who trusts my honour is the wife for me;
Your slave, your husband, and your friend employ
In search of pleasures we may both enjoy."
  To this the Damsel, meekly firm, replied:
"My mother loved, was married, toil'd, and died;
With joys she'd griefs, had troubles in her course,

But not one grief was pointed by remorse:
My mind is fix'd, to Heaven I resign,
And be her love, her life, her comforts mine."
　Tyrants have wept; and those with hearts of steel,
Unused the anguish of the heart to heal,
Have yet the transient power of virtue known,
And felt th' imparted joy promote their own.
　Our Knight relenting, now befriends a youth,
Who to the yielding maid had vow'd his truth;
And finds in that fair deed a sacred joy,
That will not perish, and that cannot cloy; -
A living joy, that shall its spirits keep,
When every beauty fades, and all the passions sleep.

PART III.

Qui vultus Acherontis atri,
Qui Stygia tristem, non tristis, videt,
. . . .
Par ille Regi, par Superis erit.
        SENECA, Agamemnon.

BURIALS.

True Christian Resignation not frequently to be seen--The Register a melancholy Record--A dying Man, who at length sends for a Priest: for what Purpose? answered--Old Collet of the Inn, an Instance of Dr Young's slow-sudden Death: his Character and Conduct--The Manners and Management of the Widow Goe: her successful Attention to Business: her Decease unexpected--the Infant Boy of Gerard Ablett dies: Reflections on his Death, and the Survivor his Sister-Twin--The Funeral of the deceased Lady of the Manor described: her neglected Mansion: Undertaker and Train: the Character which her Monument will hereafter display--Burial of an Ancient Maiden: some former drawback on her Virgin Fame: Description of her House and Household: her Manners, Apprehensions, Death--Isaac Ashford, a virtuous Peasant, dies, his manly Character: Reluctance to enter the Poor-House; and why--Misfortune and Derangement of Intellect in Robin Dingley: whence they proceeded: he is not restrained by

Misery from a wandering Life: his various returns to his Parish:
his final Return--Wife of Farmer Frankford dies in Prime of Life:
Affliction in Consequence
of such Death: melancholy View of Her House &c. on her Family's
Return from her Funeral: Address to Sorrow--Leah Cousins, a
Midwife: her Character, and successful Practice: at length opposed
by Dr. Glibb: Opposition in the Parish: Argument of the Doctor; of
Leah: her Failure and Decease--Burial of Roger Cuff, a Sailor: his
Enmity to his Family; how it originated: his Experiment and its
Consequence--The Register terminates--A Bell heard: Inquiry for
whom?--The Sexton--Character of old Dibble, and the five Rectors
whom he served--Reflections--Conclusion.

THERE was, 'tis said, and I believe, a time
When humble Christians died with views sublime;
When all were ready for their faith to bleed,
But few to write or wrangle for their creed;
When lively Faith upheld the sinking heart,
And friends, assured to meet, prepared to part;
When Love felt hope, when Sorrow grew serene,
And all was comfort in the death-bed scene.
  Alas! when now the gloomy king they wait,
'Tis weakness yielding to resistless fate;
Like wretched men upon the ocean cast,
They labour hard and struggle to the last;
"Hope against hope," and wildly gaze around
In search of help that never shall be found:
Nor, till the last strong billow stops the breath,
Will they believe them in the jaws of Death!
  When these my Records I reflecting read,
And find what ills these numerous births succeed;
What powerful griefs these nuptial ties attend;

With what regret these painful journeys end;
When from the cradle to the grave I look,
Mine I conceive a melancholy book.

    Where now is perfect resignation seen?
Alas! it is not on the village-green: -
I've seldom known, though I have often read,
Of happy peasants on their dying-bed;
Whose looks proclaimed that sunshine of the breast,
That more than hope, that Heaven itself express'd.

    What I behold are feverish fits of strife,
'Twixt fears of dying and desire of life:
Those earthly hopes, that to the last endure;
Those fears, that hopes superior fail to cure;
At best a sad submission to the doom,
Which, turning from the danger, lets it come.

    Sick lies the man, bewilder'd, lost, afraid,
His spirits vanquish'd, and his strength decay'd;
No hope the friend, the nurse, the doctor lend -
"Call then a priest, and fit him for his end."
A priest is call'd; 'tis now, alas! too late,
Death enters with him at the cottage-gate;
Or time allow'd--he goes, assured to find
The self-commending, all-confiding mind;
And sighs to hear, what we may justly call
Death's common-place, the train of thought in all.

    "True I'm a sinner," feebly he begins,
"But trust in Mercy to forgive my sins:"
(Such cool confession no past crimes excite!
Such claim on Mercy seems the sinner's right!)
"I know mankind are frail, that God is just,
And pardons those who in his Mercy trust;
We're sorely tempted in a world like this -
All men have done, and I like all, amiss;

But now, if spared, it is my full intent
On all the past to ponder and repent:
Wrongs against me I pardon great and small,
And if I die, I die in peace with all."
    His merits thus and not his sins confess'd,
He speaks his hopes, and leaves to Heaven the rest.
Alas! are these the prospects, dull and cold,
That dying Christians to their priests unfold?
Or mends the prospect when th' enthusiast cries,
"I die assured!" and in a rapture dies?
    Ah, where that humble, self-abasing mind,
With that confiding spirit, shall we find;
The mind that, feeling what repentance brings,
Dejection's terrors and Contrition's stings,
Feels then the hope that mounts all care above,
And the pure joy that flows from pardoning love?
Such have I seen in Death, and much deplore,
So many dying--that I see no more:
Lo! now my Records, where I grieve to trace
How Death has triumph'd in so short a space;
Who are the dead, how died they, I relate,
And snatch some portion of their acts from fate.
With Andrew Collett we the year begin,
The blind, fat landlord of the Old Crown Inn, -
Big as his butt, and, for the selfsame use,
To take in stores of strong fermenting juice.
On his huge chair beside the fire he sate,
In revel chief, and umpire in debate;
Each night his string of vulgar tales he told,
When ale was cheap and bachelors were bold:
His heroes all were famous in their days,
Cheats were his boast, and drunkards had his praise;
"One, in three draughts, three mugs of ale took down,

As mugs were then--the champion of the Crown;
For thrice three days another lived on ale,
And knew no change but that of mild and stale;
Two thirsty soakers watch'd a vessel's side,
When he the tap, with dext'rous hand, applied;
Nor from their seats departed, till they found
That butt was out and heard the mournful sound."

  He praised a poacher, precious child of fun!
Who shot the keeper with his own spring gun;
Nor less the smuggler who th' exciseman tied,
And left him hanging at the birch-wood side,
There to expire;--but one who saw him hang
Cut the good cord--a traitor of the gang.

  His own exploits with boastful glee he told,
What ponds he emptied and what pikes he sold;
And how, when blest with sight alert and gay,
The night's amusements kept him through the day.

  He sang the praises of those times, when all
"For cards and dice, as for their drink, might call;
When justice wink'd on every jovial crew,
And ten-pins tumbled in the parson's view."

  He told, when angry wives, provoked to rail,
Or drive a third-day drunkard from his ale,
What were his triumphs, and how great the skill
That won the vex'd virago to his will;
Who raving came;--then talked in milder strain, -
Then wept, then drank, and pledged her spouse again.

  Such were his themes : how knaves o'er laws prevail,
Or, when made captives, how they fly from jail;
The young how brave, how subtle were the old:
And oaths attested all that Folly told.

  On death like his what name shall we bestow,
So very sudden! yet so very slow?

'Twas slow: --Disease, augmenting year by year,
Show'd the grim king by gradual steps brought near:
'Twas not less sudden; in the night he died,
He drank, he swore, he jested, and he lied;
Thus aiding folly with departing breath: -
"Beware, Lorenzo, the slow-sudden death."
  Next died the Widow Goe, an active dame,
Famed ten miles round, and worthy all her fame;
She lost her husband when their loves were young,
But kept her farm, her credit, and her tongue:
Full thirty years she ruled, with matchless skill,
With guiding judgment and resistless will;
Advice she scorn'd, rebellions she suppress'd,
And sons and servants bow'd at her behest.
Like that great man's, who to his Saviour came,
Were the strong words of this commanding dame; -
"Come," if she said, they came; if "Go," were gone;
And if "Do this,"--that instant it was done:
Her maidens told she was all eye and ear,
In darkness saw and could at distance hear;
No parish-business in the place could stir,
Without direction or assent from her;
In turn she took each office as it fell,
Knew all their duties and discharged them well;
The lazy vagrants in her presence shook,
And pregnant damsels fear'd her stern rebuke;
She look'd on want with judgment clear and cool,
And felt with reason and bestow'd by rule;
She match'd both sons and daughters to her mind,
And lent them eyes, for Love, she heard, was blind;
Yet ceaseless still she throve, alert, alive,
The working bee, in full or empty hive;
Busy and careful, like that working bee,

No time for love nor tender cares had she;
But when our farmers made their amorous vows,
She talk'd of market-steeds and patent-ploughs.
Not unemploy'd her evenings pass'd away,
Amusement closed, as business waked the day;
When to her toilet's brief concern she ran,
And conversation with her friends began,
Who all were welcome, what they saw, to share;
And joyous neighbours praised her Christmas fare,
That none around might, in their scorn, complain
Of Gossip Goe as greedy in her gain.
　Thus long she reign'd, admired, if not approved;
Praised, if not honour'd; fear'd, if not beloved; -
When, as the busy days of Spring drew near,
That call'd for all the forecast of the year;
When lively hope the rising crops surveyed,
And April promised what September paid;
When stray'd her lambs where gorse and greenwood grow;
When rose her grass in richer vales below;
When pleased she look'd on all the smiling land,
And view'd the hinds, who wrought at her command;
(Poultry in groups still follow'd where she went;)
Then dread o'ercame her,--that her days were spent.
　"Bless me! I die, and not a warning giv'n, -
With MUCH to do on Earth, and ALL for Heav'n? -
No reparation for my soul's affairs,
No leave petition'd for the barn's repairs;
Accounts perplex'd, my interest yet unpaid,
My mind unsettled, and my will unmade; -
A lawyer haste, and in your way, a priest;
And let me die in one good work at least."
She spake, and, trembling, dropp'd upon her knees,
Heaven in her eye and in her hand her keys;

And still the more she found her life decay,
With greater force she grasp'd those signs of sway:
Then fell and died!--In haste her sons drew near,
And dropp'd, in haste, the tributary tear;
Then from th' adhering clasp the keys unbound,
And consolation for their sorrows found.

   Death has his infant-train; his bony arm
Strikes from the baby-cheek the rosy charm;
The brightest eye his glazing film makes dim,
And his cold touch sets fast the lithest limb:
He seized the sick'ning boy to Gerard lent,
When three days' life, in feeble cries, were spent;
In pain brought forth, those painful hours to stay,
To breathe in pain and sigh its soul away!

   "But why thus lent, if thus recall'd again,
To cause and feel, to live and die in pain?"
Or rather say, Why grevious these appear,
If all it pays for Heaven's eternal year;
If these sad sobs and piteous sighs secure
Delights that live, when worlds no more endure?

   The sister-spirit long may lodge below,
And pains from nature, pains from reason, know:
Through all the common ills of life may run,
By hope perverted and by love undone;
A wife's distress, a mother's pangs, may dread,
And widow-tears, in bitter anguish, shed;
May at old age arrive through numerous harms,
With children's children in those feeble arms:
Nor till by years of want and grief oppress'd
Shall the sad spirit flee and be at rest!

   Yet happier therefore shall we deem the boy,
Secured from anxious care and dangerous joy?

   Not so! for then would Love Divine in vain

Send all the burthens weary men sustain;
All that now curb the passions when they rage,
The checks of youth and the regrets of age;
All that now bid us hope, believe, endure,
Our sorrow's comfort and our vice's cure;
All that for Heaven's high joys the spirits train,
And charity, the crown of all, were vain.
   Say, will you call the breathless infant blest,
Because no cares the silent grave molest?
So would you deem the nursling from the wing
Untimely thrust and never train'd to sing;
But far more blest the bird whose grateful voice
Sings its own joy and makes the woods rejoice,
Though, while untaught, ere yet he charm'd the ear,
Hard were his trials and his pains severe!
   Next died the LADY who yon Hall possess'd,
And here they brought her noble bones to rest.
In Town she dwelt;--forsaken stood the Hall:
Worms ate the floors, the tap'stry fled the wall:
No fire the kitchen's cheerless grate display'd;
No cheerful light the long-closed sash convey'd:
The crawling worm, that turns a summer fly,
Here spun his shroud and laid him up to die
The winter-death:- upon the bed of state,
The bat shrill shrieking woo'd his flickering mate;
To empty rooms the curious came no more;
From empty cellars turn'd the angry poor,
And surly beggars cursed the ever-bolted door.
To one small room the steward found his way
Where tenants follow'd to complain and pay;
Yet no complaint before the Lady came,
The feeling servant spared the feeble dame;
Who saw her farms with his observing eyes,

And answer'd all requests with his replies; -
She came not down, her falling groves to view;
Why should she know, what one so faithful knew?
Why come, from many clamorous tongues to hear,
What one so just might whisper in her ear?
Her oaks or acres, why with care explore;
Why learn the wants, the sufferings of the poor;
When one so knowing all their worth could trace,
And one so piteous govern'd in her place?
  Lo! now, what dismal Sons of Darkness come,
To bear this Daughter of Indulgence home;
Tragedians all, and well-arranged in black!
Who nature, feeling, force, expression lack;
Who cause no tear, but gloomily pass by,
And shake their sables in the wearied eye,
That turns disgusted from the pompous scene,
Proud without grandeur, with profusion, mean
The tear for kindness past affection owes;
For worth deceased the sigh from reason flows
E'en well feign'd passion for our sorrows call,
And real tears for mimic miseries fall:
But this poor farce has neither truth nor art,
To please the fancy or to touch the heart;
Unlike the darkness of the sky, that pours
On the dry ground its fertilizing showers;
Unlike to that which strikes the soul with dread,
When thunders roar and forky fires are shed;
Dark but not awful, dismal but yet mean,
With anxious bustle moves the cumbrous scene;
Presents no objects tender or profound,
But spreads its cold unmeaning gloom around.
  When woes are feign'd, how ill such forms appear,
And oh! how needless, when the woe's sincere.

Slow to the vault they come, with heavy tread,
Bending beneath the Lady and her lead;
A case of elm surrounds that ponderous chest,
Close on that case the crimson velvet's press'd;
Ungenerous this, that to the worm denies,
With niggard-caution, his appointed prize;
For now, ere yet he works his tedious way,
Through cloth and wood and metal to his prey,
That prey dissolving shall a mass remain,
That fancy loathes and worms themselves disdain.
  But see! the master-mourner makes his way,
To end his office for the coffin'd clay;
Pleased that our rustic men and maids behold
His plate like silver, and his studs like gold,
As they approach to spell the age, the name,
And all the titles of the illustrious dame.-
This as (my duty done) some scholar read,
A Village-father look'd disdain and said:
"Away, my friends! why take such pains to know
What some brave marble soon in church shall show?
Where not alone her gracious name shall stand,
But how she lived--the blessing of the land;
How much we all deplored the noble dead,
What groans we utter'd and what tears we shed;
Tears, true as those which in the sleepy eyes
Of weeping cherubs on the stone shall rise;
Tears, true as those which, ere she found her grave,
The noble Lady to our sorrows gave."
  Down by the church-way walk, and where the brook
Winds round the chancel like a shepherd's crook;
In that small house, with those green pales before,
Where jasmine trails on either side the door;
Where those dark shrubs, that now grow wild at will,

Were clipped in form and tantalised with skill;
Where cockles blanch'd and pebbles neatly spread,
Form'd shining borders for the larkspurs' bed;
There lived a Lady, wise, austere, and nice,
Who show'd her virtue by her scorn of vice;
In the dear fashions of her youth she dress'd,
A pea-green Joseph was her favourite vest;
Erect she stood, she walk'd with stately mien,
Tight was her length of stays, and she was tall and lean.
   There long she lived in maiden-state immured,
From looks of love and treacherous man secured;
Though evil fame--(but that was long before)
Had blown her dubious blast at Catherine's door:
A Captain thither, rich from India came,
And though a cousin call'd, it touch'd her fame:
Her annual stipend rose from his behest,
And all the long-prized treasures she possess'd:-
If aught like joy awhile appear'd to stay
In that stern face, and chase those frowns away,
'Twas when her treasures she disposed for view
And heard the praises to their splendour due;
Silks beyond price, so rich, they'd stand alone,
And diamonds blazing on the buckled zone;
Rows of rare pearls by curious workmen set,
And bracelets fair in box of glossy jet;
Bright polish'd amber precious from its size,
Or forms the fairest fancy could devise:
Her drawers of cedar, shut with secret springs,
Conceal'd the watch of gold and rubied rings;
Letters, long proofs of love, and verses fine
Round the pink'd rims of crisped Valentine.
Her china-closet, cause of daily care,
For woman's wonder held her pencill'd ware;

That pictured wealth of China and Japan,
Like its cold mistress, shunn'd the eye of man.
　Her neat small room, adorn'd with maiden-taste,
A clipp'd French puppy, first of favourites, graced:
A parrot next, but dead and stuff'd with art;
(For Poll, when living, lost the Lady's heart,
And then his life; for he was heard to speak
Such frightful words as tinged his Lady's cheek:)
Unhappy bird! who had no power to prove,
Save by such speech, his gratitude and love.
A gray old cat his whiskers lick'd beside;
A type of sadness in the house of pride.
The polish'd surface of an India chest,
A glassy globe, in frame of ivory, press'd;
Where swam two finny creatures; one of gold,
Of silver one; both beauteous to behold:-
All these were form'd the guiding taste to suit;
The beast well-manner'd and the fishes mute.
A widow'd Aunt was there, compell'd by need
The nymph to flatter and her tribe to feed;
Who veiling well her scorn, endured the clog,
Mute as the fish and fawning as the dog.
　As years increased, these treasures, her delight,
Arose in value in their owner's sight:
A miser knows that, view it as he will,
A guinea kept is but a guinea still;
And so he puts it to its proper use,
That something more this guinea may produce;
But silks and rings, in the possessor's eyes,
The oft'ner seen, the more in value rise,
And thus are wisely hoarded to bestow
The kind of pleasure that with years will grow.
　But what avail'd their worth--if worth had they -

In the sad summer of her slow decay?
   Then we beheld her turn an anxious look
From trunks and chests, and fix it on her book, -
A rich-bound Book of Prayer the Captain gave,
(Some Princess had it, or was said to have;)
And then once more on all her stores look round,
And draw a sigh so piteous and profound,
That told, "Alas! how hard from these to part,
And for new hopes and habits form the heart!
What shall I do (she cried,) my peace of mind
To gain in dying, and to die resign'd?"
"Hear," we return'd;--"these baubles cast aside,
Nor give thy God a rival in thy pride;
Thy closets shut, and ope thy kitchen's door;
There own thy failings, here invite the poor;
A friend of Mammon let thy bounty make;
For widows' prayers, thy vanities forsake;
And let the hungry of thy pride partake:
Then shall thy inward eye with joy survey
The angel Mercy tempering Death's delay!"
   Alas! 'twas hard; the treasures still had charms,
Hope still its flattery, sickness its alarms;
Still was the same unsettled, clouded view,
And the same plaintive cry, "What shall I do?"
   Nor change appear'd; for when her race was run,
Doubtful we all exclaim'd, "What has been done?"
Apart she lived, and still she lies alone;
Yon earthy heap awaits the flattering stone
On which invention shall be long employ'd,
To show the various worth of Catherine Lloyd.
   Next to these ladies, but in nought allied,
A noble Peasant, Isaac Ashford, died.
Noble he was, contemning all things mean,

His truth unquestion'd and his soul serene:
Of no man's presence Isaac felt afraid;
At no man's question Isaac looked dismay'd:
Shame knew him not, he dreaded no disgrace;
Truth, simple truth, was written in his face:
Yet while the serious thought his soul approved,
Cheerful he seem'd, and gentleness he loved;
To bliss domestic he his heart resign'd,
And with the firmest had the fondest mind;
Were others joyful, he look'd smiling on,
And gave allowance where he needed none;
Good he refused with future ill to buy,
Nor knew a joy that caused reflection's sigh;
A friend to virtue, his unclouded breast
No envy stung, no jealousy distress'd;
(Bane of the poor! it wounds their weaker mind,
To miss one favour, which their neighbours find:)
Yet far was he from stoic pride removed;
He felt humanely, and he warmly loved:
I mark'd his action, when his infant died,
And his old neighbour for offence was tried;
The still tears, stealing down that furrow'd cheek,
Spoke pity, plainer than the tongue can speak.
If pride were his, 'twas not their vulgar pride,
Who, in their base contempt, the great deride;
Nor pride in learning,--though my Clerk agreed,
If fate should call him, Ashford might succeed;
Nor pride in rustic skill, although we knew
None his superior, and his equals few:-
But if that spirit in his soul had place,
It was the jealous pride that shuns disgrace;
A pride in honest fame, by virtue gain'd,
In sturdy boys to virtuous labours train'd;

Pride in the power that guards his country's coast,
And all that Englishmen enjoy and boast;
Pride in a life that slander's tongue defied, -
In fact a noble passion, misnamed Pride.
    He had no party's rage, no sect'ry's whim;
Christian and countrymen was all with him:
True to his church he came; no Sunday-shower
Kept him at home in that important hour;
Nor his firm feet could one persuading sect,
By the strong glare of their new light direct:-
"On hope, in mine own sober light, I gaze,
But should be blind, and lose it, in your blaze."
    In times severe, when many a sturdy swain
Felt it his pride, his comfort to complain;
Isaac their wants would soothe, his own would hide,
And feel in that his comfort and his pride.
    At length he found when seventy years were run,
His strength departed, and his labour done;
When he, save honest fame, retain'd no more,
But lost his wife, and saw his children poor:
'Twas then a spark of--say not discontent -
Struck on his mind, and thus he gave it vent:-
    "Kind are your laws ('tis not to be denied,)
That in yon House for ruin'd age provide,
And they are just;--when young we give you all,
And for assistance in our weakness call.-
Why then this proud reluctance to be fed,
To join your poor, and eat the parish bread?
But yet I linger, loth with him to feed,
Who gains his plenty by the sons of need;
He who, by contract, all your paupers took,
And gauges stomachs with an anxious look:
On some old master I could well depend;

See him with joy and thank him as a friend;
But ill on him who doles the day's supply,
And counts our chances who at night may die:
Yet help me, Heav'n! and let me not complain
Of what I suffer, but my fate sustain."

   Such were his thoughts, and so resign'd he grew;
Daily he placed the Workhouse in his view!
But came not there, for sudden was his fate,
He dropp'd, expiring, at his cottage gate.

   I feel his absence in the hours of prayer,
And view his seat, and sigh for Isaac there:
I see no more these white locks thinly spread
Round the bald polish of that honour'd head;
No more that awful glance on playful wight,
Compell'd to kneel and tremble at the sight,
To fold his fingers, all in dread the while,
Till Mister Ashford soften'd to a smile;
No more that meek and suppliant look in prayer,
Nor the pure faith (to give it force), are there: -
But he is blest, and I lament no more
A wise good man contented to be poor.

   Then died a Rambler: not the one who sails,
And trucks, for female favours, beads and nails;
Not one who posts from place to place--of men
And manners treating with a flying pen;
Not he who climbs, for prospects, Snowdon's height,
And chides the clouds that intercept the sight;
No curious shell, rare plant, or brilliant spar,
Enticed our traveller from his house so far;
But all the reason by himself assign'd
For so much rambling, was a restless mind;
As on, from place to place, without intent,
Without reflection, Robin Dingley went.

Not thus by nature:- never man was found
Less prone to wander from his parish bound:
Claudian's Old Man, to whom all scenes were new,
Save those where he and where his apples grew,
Resembled Robin, who around would look,
And his horizon for the earth's mistook.
    To this poor swain a keen Attorney came; -
"I give thee joy, good fellow! on thy name;
The rich old Dingley's dead;--no child has he,
Nor wife, nor will; his ALL is left for thee:
To be his fortune's heir thy claim is good;
Thou hast the name, and we will prove the blood."
The claim was made; 'twas tried,--it would not stand;
They proved the blood but were refused the land.
Assured of wealth, this man of simple heart
To every friend had predisposed a part;
His wife had hopes indulged of various kind;
The three Miss Dingleys had their school assign'd,
Masters were sought for what they each required,
And books were bought and harpsichords were hired;
So high was hope:- the failure touched his brain,
And Robin never was himself again;
Yet he no wrath, no angry wish express'd,
But tried, in vain, to labour or to rest;
Then cast his bundle on his back, and went
He knew not whither, nor for what intent.
    Years fled;--of Robin all remembrance past,
When home he wandered in his rags at last:
A sailor's jacket on his limbs was thrown,
A sailor's story he had made his own;
Had suffer'd battles, prisons, tempests, storms,
Encountering death in all its ugliest forms:
His cheeks were haggard, hollow was his eye,

Where madness lurk'd, conceal'd in misery;
Want, and th' ungentle world, had taught a part,
And prompted cunning to that simple heart:
"He now bethought him, he would roam no more
But live at home and labour as before."
   Here clothed and fed, no sooner he began
To round and redden, than away he ran;
His wife was dead, their children past his aid,
So, unmolested, from his home he stray'd:
Six years elapsed, when, worn with want and pain.
Came Robin, wrapt in all his rags again:
We chide, we pity;--placed among our poor,
He fed again, and was a man once more.
   As when a gaunt and hungry fox is found,
Entrapp'd alive in some rich hunter's ground;
Fed for the field, although each day's a feast,
FATTEN you may, but never TAME the beast;
A house protects him, savoury viands sustain:-
But loose his neck and off he goes again:
So stole our Vagrant from his warm retreat,
To rove a prowler and be deemed a cheat.
   Hard was his fare; for him at length we saw
In cart convey'd and laid supine on straw.
His feeble voice now spoke a sinking heart;
His groans now told the motions of the cart:
And when it stopp'd, he tried in vain to stand;
Closed was his eye, and clench'd his clammy hand:
Life ebb'd apace, and our best aid no more
Could his weak sense or dying heart restore:
But now he fell, a victim to the snare
That vile attorneys for the weak prepare;
They who when profit or resentment call,
Heed not the groaning victim they enthrall.

Then died lamented in the strength of life,
A valued MOTHER and a faithful WIFE;
Call'd not away when time had loosed each hold
On the fond heart, and each desire grew cold;
But when, to all that knit us to our kind,
She felt fast-bound, as charity can bind; -
Not when the ills of age, its pain, its care,
The drooping spirit for its fate prepare;
And, each affection failing, leaves the heart
Loosed from life's charm, and willing to depart;
But all her ties the strong invader broke,
In all their strength, by one tremendous stroke!
Sudden and swift the eager pest came on,
And terror grew, till every hope was gone;
Still those around appear'd for hope to seek!
But view'd the sick and were afraid to speak.
   Slowly they bore, with solemn step, the dead;
When grief grew loud and bitter tears were shed,
My part began; a crowd drew near the place,
Awe in each eye, alarm in every face:
So swift the ill, and of so fierce a kind,
That fear with pity mingled in each mind;
Friends with the husband came their griefs to blend,
For good-man Frankford was to all a friend.
The last-born boy they held above the bier,
He knew not grief, but cries express'd his fear;
Each different age and sex reveal'd its pain,
In now a louder, now a lower strain;
While the meek father listening to their tones,
Swell'd the full cadence of the grief by groans.
   The elder sister strove her pangs to hide,
And soothing words to younger minds applied'.
"Be still, be patient;" oft she strove to stay;

But fail'd as oft, and weeping turn'd away.
  Curious and sad, upon the fresh-dug hill
The village lads stood melancholy still;
And idle children, wandering to and fro.
As Nature guided, took the tone of woe.
  Arrived at home, how then they gazed around
On every place--where she no more was found; -
The seat at table she was wont to fill;
The fire-side chair, still set, but vacant still;
The garden-walks, a labour all her own;
The latticed bower, with trailing shrubs o'ergrown,
The Sunday-pew she fill'd with all her race, -
Each place of hers, was now a sacred place
That, while it call'd up sorrows in the eyes,
Pierced the full heart and forced them still to rise.
  Oh sacred sorrow! by whom souls are tried,
Sent not to punish mortals, but to guide;
If thou art mine (and who shall proudly dare
To tell his Maker, he has had a share!)
Still let me feel for what thy pangs are sent,
And be my guide, and not my punishment!
  Of Leah Cousins next the name appears,
With honours crown'd and blest with length of years,
Save that she lived to feel, in life's decay,
The pleasure die, the honours drop away;
A matron she, whom every village-wife
View'd as the help and guardian of her life,
Fathers and sons, indebted to her aid,
Respect to her and her profession paid;
Who in the house of plenty largely fed,
Yet took her station at the pauper's bed;
Nor from that duty could be bribed again,
While fear or danger urged her to remain:

In her experience all her friends relied.
Heaven was her help and nature was her guide.
   Thus Leah lived; long trusted, much caress'd,
Till a Town-Dame a youthful farmer bless'd;
A gay vain bride, who would example give
To that poor village where she deign'd to live;
Some few months past, she sent, in hour of need,
For Doctor Glibb, who came with wond'rous speed,
Two days he waited, all his art applied,
To save the mother when her infant died: -
"'Twas well I came," at last he deign'd to say;
"'Twas wondrous well;"--and proudly rode away.
   The news ran round;--"How vast the Doctor's pow'r!"
He saved the Lady in the trying hour;
Saved her from death, when she was dead to hope,
And her fond husband had resign'd her up:
So all, like her, may evil fate defy,
If Doctor Glibb, with saving hand, be nigh.
   Fame (now his friend), fear, novelty, and whim,
And fashion, sent the varying sex to him:
From this, contention in the village rose;
And these the Dame espoused; the Doctor those,
The wealthier part to him and science went;
With luck and her the poor remain'd content.
   The Matron sigh'd; for she was vex'd at heart,
With so much profit, so much fame, to part:
"So long successful in my art," she cried,
"And this proud man, so young and so untried!"
"Nay," said the Doctor, "dare you trust your wives,
The joy, the pride, the solace of your lives,
To one who acts and knows no reason why,
But trusts, poor hag! to luck for an ally? -
Who, on experience, can her claims advance,

And own the powers of accident and chance?
A whining dame, who prays in danger's view,
(A proof she knows not what beside to do;)
What's her experience? In the time that's gone,
Blundering she wrought, and still she blunders on:-
And what is Nature? One who acts in aid
Of gossips half asleep and half afraid:
With such allies I scorn my fame to blend,
Skill is my luck and courage is my friend:
No slave to Nature, 'tis my chief delight
To win my way and act in her despite:-
Trust then my art, that, in itself complete,
Needs no assistance and fears no defeat."
　　Warm'd by her well-spiced ale and aiding pipe,
The angry Matron grew for contest ripe.
　　"Can you," she said, "ungrateful and unjust,
Before experience, ostentation trust!
What is your hazard, foolish daughters, tell?
If safe, you're certain; if secure, you're well:
That I have luck must friend and foe confess,
And what's good judgment but a lucky guess?
He boasts, but what he can do: --will you run
From me, your friend! who, all lie boasts, have done?
By proud and learned words his powers are known;
By healthy boys and handsome girls my own:
Wives! fathers! children! by my help you live;
Has this pale Doctor more than life to give?
No stunted cripple hops the village round;
Your hands are active and your heads are sound;
My lads are all your fields and flocks require;
My lasses all those sturdy lads admire.
Can this proud leech, with all his boasted skill,
Amend the soul or body, wit or will?

Does he for courts the sons of farmers frame,
Or make the daughter differ from the dame?
Or, whom he brings into this world of woe,
Prepares he them their part to undergo?
If not, this stranger from your doors repel,
And be content to BE and to be WELL."
   She spake; but, ah! with words too strong and plain;
Her warmth offended, and her truth was vain:
The many left her, and the friendly few,
If never colder, yet they older grew;
Till, unemploy'd, she felt her spirits droop,
And took, insidious aid! th' inspiring cup;
Grew poor and peevish as her powers decay'd,
And propp'd the tottering frame with stronger aid,
Then died! I saw our careful swains convey,
From this our changeful world, the Matron's clay,
Who to this world, at least, with equal care,
Brought them its changes, good and ill, to share.
   Now to his grave was Roger Cuff conveyed,
And strong resentment's lingering spirit laid.
Shipwreck'd in youth, he home return'd, and found
His brethren three--and thrice they wish'd him drown'd.
"Is this a landsman's love? Be certain then,
"We part for ever!"--and they cried, "Amen!"
   His words were truth's:- Some forty summers fled,
His brethren died; his kin supposed him dead:
Three nephews these, one sprightly niece, and one,
Less near in blood--they call'd him surly John;
He work'd in woods apart from all his kind,
Fierce were his looks and moody was his mind.
   For home the sailor now began to sigh:-
"The dogs are dead, and I'll return and die;
When all I have, my gains, in years of care,

The younger Cuffs with kinder souls shall share -
Yet hold! I'm rich;--with one consent they'll say,
'You're welcome, Uncle, as the flowers in May.'
No; I'll disguise me, be in tatters dress'd,
And best befriend the lads who treat me best."
   Now all his kindred,--neither rich nor poor, -
Kept the wolf want some distance from the door.
   In piteous plight he knock'd at George's gate,
And begg'd for aid, as he described his state:-
But stern was George;--"Let them who had thee strong,
Help thee to drag thy weaken'd frame along;
To us a stranger, while your limbs would move,
From us depart, and try a stranger's love:-
"Ha! dost thou murmur?"--for, in Roger's throat,
Was "Rascal!" rising with disdainful note.
   To pious James he then his prayer address'd; -
"Good-lack," quoth James, "thy sorrows pierce my breast
And, had I wealth, as have my brethren twain,
One board should feed us and one roof contain:
But plead I will thy cause, and I will pray:
And so farewell! Heaven help thee on thy way!"
"Scoundrel!" said Roger (but apart);--and told
His case to Peter;--Peter too was cold;
"The rates are high; we have a-many poor;
But I will think,"--he said, and shut the door.
   Then the gay niece the seeming pauper press'd; -
"Turn, Nancy, turn, and view this form distress'd:
Akin to thine is this declining frame,
And this poor beggar claims an Uncle's name."
   "Avaunt! begone!" the courteous maiden said,
"Thou vile impostor! Uncle Roger's dead:
I hate thee, beast; thy look my spirit shocks;
Oh! that I saw thee starving in the stocks!"

"My gentle niece!" he said--and sought the wood,
"I hunger, fellow; prithee, give me food!"
  "Give! am I rich? This hatchet take, and try
Thy proper strength, nor give those limbs the lie;
Work, feed thyself, to thine own powers appeal,
Nor whine out woes thine own right-hand can heal;
And while that hand is thine, and thine a leg,
Scorn of the proud or of the base to beg."
  "Come, surly John, thy wealthy kinsman view,"
Old Roger said;--"thy words are brave and true;
Come, live with me: we'll vex those scoundrel-boys,
And that prim shrew shall, envying, hear our joys. -
Tobacco's glorious fume all day we'll share,
With beef and brandy kill all kinds of care;
We'll beer and biscuit on our table heap,
And rail at rascals, till we fall asleep."
  Such was their life; but when the woodman died,
His grieving kin for Roger's smiles applied -
In vain; he shut, with stern rebuke, the door,
And dying, built a refuge for the poor,
With this restriction, That no Cuff should share
One meal, or shelter for one moment there.
  My Record ends:- But hark! e'en now I hear
The bell of death, and know not whose to fear:
Our farmers all, and all our hinds were well;
In no man's cottage danger seem'd to dwell: -
Yet death of man proclaim these heavy chimes,
For thrice they sound, with pausing space, three times,
  "Go; of my Sexton seek, Whose days are sped? -
What! he, himself!- and is old Dibble dead?"
His eightieth year he reach'd, still undecay d,
And rectors five to one close vault convey'd:-
But he is gone; his care and skill I lose,

And gain a mournful subject for my Muse:
His masters lost, he'd oft in turn deplore,
And kindly add,--"Heaven grant, I lose no more!"
Yet, while he spake, a sly and pleasant glance
Appear'd at variance with his complaisance:
For, as he told their fate and varying worth,
He archly look'd,--"I yet may bear thee forth."
"When first"--(he so began)--"my trade I plied,
Good master Addle was the parish-guide;
His clerk and sexton, I beheld with fear,
His stride majestic, and his frown severe;
A noble pillar of the church he stood,
Adorn'd with college-gown and parish hood:
Then as he paced the hallow'd aisles about,
He fill'd the seven-fold surplice fairly out!
But in his pulpit wearied down with prayer,
He sat and seem'd as in his study's chair;
For while the anthem swell'd, and when it ceased,
Th'expecting people view'd their slumbering priest;
Who, dozing, died.--Our Parson Peele was next;
'I will not spare you,' was his favourite text;
Nor did he spare, but raised them many a pound;
E'en me he mulct for my poor rood of ground;
Yet cared he nought, but with a gibing speech,
'What should I do,' quoth he, 'but what I preach?'
His piercing jokes (and he'd a plenteous store)
Were daily offer'd both to rich and poor;
His scorn, his love, in playful words he spoke;
His pity, praise, and promise, were a joke:
But though so young and blest with spirits high,
He died as grave as any judge could die:
The strong attack subdued his lively powers, -
His was the grave, and Doctor Grandspear ours.

"Then were there golden times the village round;
In his abundance all appear'd t'abound;
Liberal and rich, a plenteous board he spread,
E'en cool Dissenters at his table fed;
Who wish'd and hoped,--and thought a man so kind
A way to Heaven, though not their own, might find.
To them, to all, he was polite and free,
Kind to the poor, and, ah! most kind to me!
'Ralph,' would he say, 'Ralph Dibble, thou art old;
That doublet fit, 'twill keep thee from the cold:
How does my sexton?- What! the times are hard;
Drive that stout pig, and pen him in thy yard.'
But most, his rev'rence loved a mirthful jest:-
'Thy coat is thin; why, man, thou'rt BARELY dress'd
It's worn to th' thread: but I have nappy beer;
Clap that within, and see how they will wear!'
    "Gay days were these; but they were quickly past:
When first he came, we found he couldn't last:
A whoreson cough (and at the fall of leaf)
Upset him quite;--but what's the gain of grief?
    "Then came the Author-Rector: his delight
Was all in books; to read them or to write:
Women and men he strove alike to shun,
And hurried homeward when his tasks were done;
Courteous enough, but careless what he said,
For points of learning he reserved his head;
And when addressing either poor or rich,
He knew no better than his cassock which:
He, like an osier, was of pliant kind,
Erect by nature, but to bend inclined;
Not like a creeper falling to the ground,
Or meanly catching on the neighbours round:
Careless was he of surplice, hood, and band, -

And kindly took them as they came to hand,
Nor, like the doctor, wore a world of hat,
As if he sought for dignity in that:
He talk'd, he gave, but not with cautious rules;
Nor turn'd from gipsies, vagabonds, or fools;
It was his nature, but they thought it whim,
And so our beaux and beauties turn'd from him.
Of questions, much he wrote, profound and dark, -
How spake the serpent, and where stopp'd the ark;
From what far land the queen of Sheba came;
Who Salem's Priest, and what his father's name;
He made the Song of Songs its mysteries yield,
And Revelations to the world reveal'd.
He sleeps i' the aisle,--but not a stone records
His name or fame, his actions or his words:
And truth, your reverence, when I look around,
And mark the tombs in our sepulchral ground
(Though dare I not of one man's hope to doubt),
I'd join the party who repose without.
  "Next came a Youth from Cambridge, and in truth
He was a sober and a comely youth;
He blush'd in meekness as a modest man,
And gain'd attention ere his task began;
When preaching, seldom ventured on reproof,
But touch'd his neighbours tenderly enough.
Him, in his youth, a clamorous sect assail'd,
Advised and censured, flatter'd,--and prevail'd.-
Then did he much his sober hearers vex,
Confound the simple, and the sad perplex;
To a new style his reverence rashly took;
Loud grew his voice, to threat'ning swell'd his look;
Above, below, on either side, he gazed,
Amazing all, and most himself amazed:

No more he read his preachments pure and plain,
But launch'd outright, and rose and sank again:
At times he smiled in scorn, at times he wept,
And such sad coil with words of vengeance kept,
That our blest sleepers started as they slept.
  'Conviction comes like light'ning,' he would cry;
'In vain you seek it, and in vain you fly;
'Tis like the rushing of the mighty wind,
Unseen its progress, but its power you find;
It strikes the child ere yet its reason wakes;
His reason fled, the ancient sire it shakes;
The proud, learn'd man, and him who loves to know
How and from whence those gusts of grace will blow,
It shuns,--but sinners in their way impedes,
And sots and harlots visits in their deeds:
Of faith and penance it supplies the place;
Assures the vilest that they live by grace,
And, without running, makes them win the race.'
  "Such was the doctrine our young prophet taught;
And here conviction, there confusion wrought;
When his thin cheek assumed a deadly hue,
And all the rose to one small spot withdrew,
They call'd it hectic; 'twas a fiery flush,
More fix'd and deeper than the maiden blush;
His paler lips the pearly teeth disclosed,
And lab'ring lungs the length'ning speech opposed.
No more his span-girth shanks and quiv'ring thighs
Upheld a body of the smaller size;
But down he sank upon his dying bed,
And gloomy crotchets fill'd his wandering head.
  'Spite of my faith, all-saving faith,' he cried,
'I fear of worldly works the wicked pride;
Poor as I am, degraded, abject, blind,

The good I've wrought still rankles in my mind;
My alms-deeds all, and every deed I've done;
My moral-rags defile me every one;
It should not be:- what say'st thou! tell me, Ralph.'
Quoth I, 'Your reverence, I believe, you're safe;
Your faith's your prop, nor have you pass'd such time
In life's good-works as swell them to a crime.
If I of pardon for my sins were sure,
About my goodness I would rest secure.'
  "Such was his end; and mine approaches fast;
I've seen my best of preachers,--and my last," -
  He bow'd, and archly smiled at what he said,
Civil but sly:- "And is old Dibble dead?"
  Yes; he is gone: and WE are going all;
Like flowers we wither, and like leaves we fall; -
Here, with an infant, joyful sponsors come,
Then bear the new-made Christian to its home:
A few short years and we behold him stand
To ask a blessing, with his bride in hand:
A few, still seeming shorter, and we hear
His widow weeping at her husband's bier:-
Thus, as the months succeed, shall infants take
Their names; thus parents shall the child forsake;
Thus brides again and bridegrooms blithe shall kneel,
By love or law compell'd their vows to seal,
Ere I again, or one like me, explore
These simple Annals of the VILLAGE POOR.

1801.

The Codes Of Hammurabi And Moses
W. W. Davies

QTY

The discovery of the Hammurabi Code is one of the greatest achievements of archaeology, and is of paramount interest, not only to the student of the Bible, but also to all those interested in ancient history...

Religion   ISBN: *1-59462-338-4*   Pages:132

MSRP $12.95

The Theory of Moral Sentiments
Adam Smith

QTY

This work from 1749. contains original theories of conscience amd moral judgment and it is the foundation for systemof morals.

Philosophy ISBN: *1-59462-777-0*   Pages:536

MSRP $19.95

Jessica's First Prayer
Hesba Stretton

QTY

In a screened and secluded corner of one of the many railway-bridges which span the streets of London there could be seen a few years ago, from five o'clock every morning until half past eight, a tidily set-out coffee-stall, consisting of a trestle and board, upon which stood two large tin cans, with a small fire of charcoal burning under each so as to keep the coffee boiling during the early hours of the morning when the work-people were thronging into the city on their way to their daily toil...

Childrens   ISBN: *1-59462-373-2*

Pages:84

MSRP $9.95

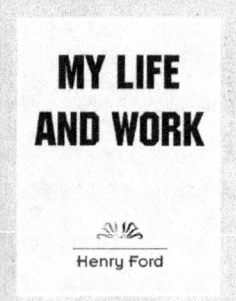

My Life and Work
Henry Ford

QTY

Henry Ford revolutionized the world with his implementation of mass production for the Model T automobile. Gain valuable business insight into his life and work with his own auto-biography... "We have only started on our development of our country we have not as yet, with all our talk of wonderful progress, done more than scratch the surface. The progress has been wonderful enough but..."

Biographies/   ISBN: *1-59462-198-5*

Pages:300

MSRP $21.95

The Art of Cross-Examination
Francis Wellman

QTY

I presume it is the experience of every author, after his first book is published upon an important subject, to be almost overwhelmed with a wealth of ideas and illustrations which could readily have been included in his book, and which to his own mind, at least, seem to make a second edition inevitable. Such certainly was the case with me; and when the first edition had reached its sixth impression in five months, I rejoiced to learn that it seemed to my publishers that the book had met with a sufficiently favorable reception to justify a second and considerably enlarged edition. ..

Reference   ISBN: *1-59462-647-2*

Pages:412

MSRP *$19.95*

On the Duty of Civil Disobedience
Henry David Thoreau

QTY

Thoreau wrote his famous essay, On the Duty of Civil Disobedience, as a protest against an unjust but popular war and the immoral but popular institution of slave-owning. He did more than write—he declined to pay his taxes, and was hauled off to gaol in consequence. Who can say how much this refusal of his hastened the end of the war and of slavery ?

Law   ISBN: *1-59462-747-9*

Pages:48

MSRP *$7.45*

Dream Psychology Psychoanalysis for Beginners
Sigmund Freud

QTY

Sigmund Freud, born Sigismund Schlomo Freud (May 6, 1856 - September 23, 1939), was a Jewish-Austrian neurologist and psychiatrist who co-founded the psychoanalytic school of psychology. Freud is best known for his theories of the unconscious mind, especially involving the mechanism of repression; his redefinition of sexual desire as mobile and directed towards a wide variety of objects; and his therapeutic techniques, especially his understanding of transference in the therapeutic relationship and the presumed value of dreams as sources of insight into unconscious desires.

Psychology   ISBN: *1-59462-905-6*

Pages:196

MSRP *$15.45*

The Miracle of Right Thought
Orison Swett Marden

QTY

Believe with all of your heart that you will do what you were made to do. When the mind has once formed the habit of holding cheerful, happy, prosperous pictures, it will not be easy to form the opposite habit. It does not matter how improbable or how far away this realization may see, or how dark the prospects may be, if we visualize them as best we can, as vividly as possible, hold tenaciously to them and vigorously struggle to attain them, they will gradually become actualized, realized in the life. But a desire, a longing without endeavor, a yearning abandoned or held indifferently will vanish without realization.

Self Help   ISBN: *1-59462-644-8*

Pages:360

MSRP *$25.45*

QTY

The Rosicrucian Cosmo-Conception Mystic Christianity by *Max Heindel* ISBN: *1-59462-188-8* **$38.95**
The Rosicrucian Cosmo-conception is not dogmatic, neither does it appeal to any other authority than the reason of the student. It is: not controversial, but is: sent forth in the, hope that it may help to clear... New Age/Religion Pages 646

Abandonment To Divine Providence by *Jean-Pierre de Caussade* ISBN: *1-59462-228-0* **$25.95**
"The Rev. Jean Pierre de Caussade was one of the most remarkable spiritual writers of the Society of Jesus in France in the 18th Century. His death took place at Toulouse in 1751. His works have gone through many editions and have been republished... Inspirational/Religion Pages 400

Mental Chemistry by *Charles Haanel* ISBN: *1-59462-192-6* **$23.95**
Mental Chemistry allows the change of material conditions by combining and appropriately utilizing the power of the mind. Much like applied chemistry creates something new and unique out of careful combinations of chemicals the mastery of mental chemistry... New Age Pages 354

The Letters of Robert Browning and Elizabeth Barret Barrett 1845-1846 vol II ISBN: *1-59462-193-4* **$35.95**
by *Robert Browning and Elizabeth Barrett* Biographies Pages 596

Gleanings In Genesis (volume I) by *Arthur W. Pink* ISBN: *1-59462-130-6* **$27.45**
Appropriately has Genesis been termed "the seed plot of the Bible" for in it we have, in germ form, almost all of the great doctrines which are afterwards fully developed in the books of Scripture which follow... Religion/Inspirational Pages 420

The Master Key by *L. W. de Laurence* ISBN: *1-59462-001-6* **$30.95**
In no branch of human knowledge has there been a more lively increase of the spirit of research during the past few years than in the study of Psychology, Concentration and Mental Discipline. The requests for authentic lessons in Thought Control, Mental Discipline and... New Age/Business Pages 422

The Lesser Key Of Solomon Goetia by *L. W. de Laurence* ISBN: *1-59462-092-X* **$9.95**
This translation of the first book of the "Lernegton" which is now for the first time made accessible to students of Talismanic Magic was done, after careful collation and edition, from numerous Ancient Manuscripts in Hebrew, Latin, and French... New Age/Occult Pages 92

Rubaiyat Of Omar Khayyam by *Edward Fitzgerald* ISBN:*1-59462-332-5* **$13.95**
Edward Fitzgerald, whom the world has already learned, in spite of his own efforts to remain within the shadow of anonymity, to look upon as one of the rarest poets of the century, was born at Bredfield, in Suffolk, on the 31st of March, 1809. He was the third son of John Purcell... Music Pages 172

Ancient Law by *Henry Maine* ISBN: *1-59462-128-4* **$29.95**
The chief object of the following pages is to indicate some of the earliest ideas of mankind, as they are reflected in Ancient Law, and to point out the relation of those ideas to modern thought. Religion/History Pages 452

Far-Away Stories by *William J. Locke* ISBN: *1-59462-129-2* **$19.45**
"Good wine needs no bush, but a collection of mixed vintages does. And this book is just such a collection. Some of the stories I do not want to remain buried for ever in the museum files of dead magazine-numbers an author's not unpardonable vanity..." Fiction Pages 272

Life of David Crockett by *David Crockett* ISBN: *1-59462-250-7* **$27.45**
"Colonel David Crockett was one of the most remarkable men of the times in which he lived. Born in humble life, but gifted with a strong will, an indomitable courage, and unremitting perseverance... Biographies/New Age Pages 424

Lip-Reading by *Edward Nitchie* ISBN: *1-59462-206-X* **$25.95**
Edward B. Nitchie, founder of the New York School for the Hard of Hearing, now the Nitchie School of Lip-Reading, Inc, wrote "LIP-READING Principles and Practice". The development and perfecting of this meritorious work on lip-reading was an undertaking... How-to Pages 400

A Handbook of Suggestive Therapeutics, Applied Hypnotism, Psychic Science ISBN: *1-59462-214-0* **$24.95**
by *Henry Munro* Health/New Age/Health/Self-help Pages 376

A Doll's House: and Two Other Plays by *Henrik Ibsen* ISBN: *1-59462-112-8* **$19.95**
Henrik Ibsen created this classic when in revolutionary 1848 Rome. Introducing some striking concepts in playwriting for the realist genre, this play has been studied the world over. Fiction/Classics/Plays 308

The Light of Asia by *sir Edwin Arnold* ISBN: *1-59462-204-3* **$13.95**
In this poetic masterpiece, Edwin Arnold describes the life and teachings of Buddha. The man who was to become known as Buddha to the world was born as Prince Gautama of India but he rejected the worldly riches and abandoned the reigns of power when... Religion/History/Biographies Pages 170

The Complete Works of Guy de Maupassant by *Guy de Maupassant* ISBN: *1-59462-157-8* **$16.95**
"For days and days, nights and nights, I had dreamed of that first kiss which was to consecrate our engagement, and I knew not on what spot I should put my lips..." Fiction/Classics Pages 240

The Art of Cross-Examination by *Francis L. Wellman* ISBN: *1-59462-309-0* **$26.95**
Written by a renowned trial lawyer, Wellman imparts his experience and uses case studies to explain how to use psychology to extract desired information through questioning. How-to/Science/Reference Pages 408

Answered or Unanswered? by *Louisa Vaughan* ISBN: *1-59462-248-5* **$10.95**
Miracles of Faith in China Religion Pages 112

The Edinburgh Lectures on Mental Science (1909) by *Thomas* ISBN: *1-59462-008-3* **$11.95**
This book contains the substance of a course of lectures recently given by the writer in the Queen Street Hall, Edinburgh. Its purpose is to indicate the Natural Principles governing the relation between Mental Action and Material Conditions... New Age/Psychology Pages 148

Ayesha by *H. Rider Haggard* ISBN: *1-59462-301-5* **$24.95**
Verily and indeed it is the unexpected that happens! Probably if there was one person upon the earth from whom the Editor of this, and of a certain previous history, did not expect to hear again... Classics Pages 380

Ayala's Angel by *Anthony Trollope* ISBN: *1-59462-352-X* **$29.95**
The two girls were both pretty, but Lucy who was twenty-one who supposed to be simple and comparatively unattractive, whereas Ayala was credited, as her Bombwhat romantic name might show, with poetic charm and a taste for romance. Ayala when her father died was nineteen... Fiction Pages 484

The American Commonwealth by *James Bryce* ISBN: *1-59462-286-8* **$34.45**
An interpretation of American democratic political theory. It examines political mechanics and society from the perspective of Scotsman James Bryce Politics Pages 572

Stories of the Pilgrims by *Margaret P. Pumphrey* ISBN: *1-59462-116-0* **$17.95**
This book explores pilgrims religious oppression in England as well as their escape to Holland and eventual crossing to America on the Mayflower, and their early days in New England... History Pages 268

QTY

The Fasting Cure *by Sinclair Upton* ISBN: *1-59462-222-1* **$13.95**
In the Cosmopolitan Magazine for May, 1910, and in the Contemporary Review (London) for April, 1910, I published an article dealing with my experiences in fasting. I have written a great many magazine articles, but never one which attracted so much attention... New Age/Self Help/Health Pages 164

Hebrew Astrology *by Sepharial* ISBN: *1-59462-308-2* **$13.45**
In these days of advanced thinking it is a matter of common observation that we have left many of the old landmarks behind and that we are now pressing forward to greater heights and to a wider horizon than that which represented the mind-content of our progenitors... Astrology Pages 144

Thought Vibration or The Law of Attraction in the Thought World ISBN: *1-59462-127-6* **$12.95**

by William Walker Atkinson *Psychology/Religion Pages 144*

Optimism *by Helen Keller* ISBN: *1-59462-108-X* **$15.95**
Helen Keller was blind, deaf, and mute since 19 months old, yet famously learned how to overcome these handicaps, communicate with the world, and spread her lectures promoting optimism. An inspiring read for everyone... Biographies/Inspirational Pages 84

Sara Crewe *by Frances Burnett* ISBN: *1-59462-360-0* **$9.45**
In the first place, Miss Minchin lived in London. Her home was a large, dull, tall one, in a large, dull square, where all the houses were alike, and all the sparrows were alike, and where all the door-knockers made the same heavy sound... Childrens/Classic Pages 88

The Autobiography of Benjamin Franklin *by Benjamin Franklin* ISBN: *1-59462-135-7* **$24.95**
The Autobiography of Benjamin Franklin has probably been more extensively read than any other American historical work, and no other book of its kind has had such ups and downs of fortune. Franklin lived for many years in England, where he was agent... Biographies History Pages 332

Name	
Email	
Telephone	
Address	
City, State ZIP	

☐ **Credit Card**   ☐ **Check / Money Order**

Credit Card Number	
Expiration Date	
Signature	

Please Mail to: Book Jungle
PO Box 2226
Champaign, IL 61825
or Fax to: 630-214-0564

ORDERING INFORMATION

web*: www.bookjungle.com*
email*: sales@bookjungle.com*
fax*: 630-214-0564*
mail*: Book Jungle PO Box 2226 Champaign, IL 61825*
or PayPal *to sales@bookjungle.com*

Please contact us for bulk discounts

DIRECT-ORDER TERMS

**20% Discount if You Order
Two or More Books**
Free Domestic Shipping!
Accepted: Master Card, Visa,
Discover, American Express